NIGHTRIDER'S MOON

They killed Sheriff Fred Coffey for no apparent reason in a dead-end canyon of the high country when he was riding out to look into a report that there were three nightriders back in there. Old Jess Palmer, who was with the Sheriff at the time, brought the news back to McAllister that night. Frank Hall led the band of manhunters who rode out of town on the trail of those killers. Doc Heatly was neither a gunfighter nor a posseman, yet he scored the first kill, and during the two nights and a day he saw as much fighting as most professional possemen see in half a lifetime.

NIGHTRIDER'S MOON

John Kilgore

CHIVERS LARGE PRINT
BATH

British Library Cataloguing in Publication Data available

This Large Print edition is published by Chivers Press, England, 1993.

Published by arrangement with Robert Hale Limited.

U.K. Hardcover ISBN 0 7451 1714 7
U.K. Softcover ISBN 0 7451 1727 9

Photoset, printed and bound in Great Britain by
Redwood Press Limited, Melksham, Wiltshire

NIGHTRIDER'S MOON

CHAPTER ONE

Somewhere, out beyond the starwashed rimrocks where night lay silken and pitchblende-black, an old wolf threw back his head, reared up to his full height, and tongued at the old yellow moon. He probably expected no answer, an old wolf's call didn't have the same timbre as the cry of a young one, but whether he hoped for one or not, none came back. Only the eerie echo went fluting upwards against a lowering sky, sad and hollow and mysterious in the endless night.

Indians said that forlorn cry of an old lobo was the wail of a reincarnated spirit longing to serve his penance and leave earth behind for all time. Cowmen in their camps in the warm autumn said only that if the old devil came down any lower, to the gathering grounds for example, they'd fling his riddled old pelt over a tree limb as a warning to other gummer calf-killers.

When the moon was full coyotes tongued too, but they yapped, they rarely howled, but even when they did howl, it wasn't the same. An old wolf's cry had something to it that reached far down into the remembering blood of men, turning them restless and sometimes turning them morose; it was the undertones that went through a man, taking him all the way back to primitive times when that call meant all manner of things to superstitious people.

One old wolf could touch raw nerves in everyone who heard his wail for miles around. They didn't see him; they never would see him, but still he could do that to them.

It helped too, if the night was black, the stars far off, the air hushed and still and full of the fragrance of dying grass. Autumn was a time of smokey days and cobalt nights. Most of the work was done; cattle had been drifted down below snow-line, trail drives made up and sent along, shoes pulled off the horses which wintered on the range, hay put by for the animals which were kept close at every ranch, large or small, and the men who'd worked together all summer were beginning to break off, like leaves. Drifting on, heading for wherever cowboys went when the work was all done. Friendships which had been made—and enmities too—were sheared off clean, when the leaves turned golden and red, brilliant orange and scarlet, and one old moth-eaten lobo wolf high in the rimrocks made his forlorn howl to let folks know that summer was past; that the good times—and the bad times—were over for another year.

Indian summer came and went, sometimes lingering smokily over the mountains or lying golden out upon the prairies, but usually by the middle of October leaves fell, high-flying wedges of geese winged sturdily southward, and each morning the rind of ice upon the troughs was a little whiter, a little thicker.

In its own way autumn was as much a time for restlessness as springtime also was, but in a different way. Men roped out their private mounts from the remudas, rolled their bedrolls, stuffed saddle-pockets and threw a high salute backwards as they loped out of the ranchyard, outward bound. Some would return, some never would. Others would cross trails again the following year or the year after, hundreds of miles away in other parts of the cow country.

Autumn was a little like dying. For men heading south out of the high country, it was a period for recalling humorous, sad, embarrassing, vivid highlights of the summertime past. But it had a musty fragrance too, for no one could go back and change one single thing which had happened; not a word or a glance, or a curse. It was a time for men to reflect, rangeriders and owners both. Autumn was the time for men to total up all they had accomplished, all that they had done, and to think that they had passed another milestone; they were that much nearer the end of their individual trails.

When the moon stood full, the heavens were crystal clear and each star became something tangible in the frosty night, a man could wonder at the promise cradled up there for him; the mute assurance that time endlessly went on, and that he too was part of it. But it really took an old lobo wolf's mournful wail to bring on a silence around the cow-camp fire, bringing rough men to their private thoughts, bringing them inward to face themselves; what they had become, what they had meant instead to become, and what they were, not what they should've been.

Each autumn, like each spring and summer, brought its total changes. In the Snake River country where distance could only be measured by a long glance from some crag and where roads, when they existed at all, ran close to settlements, smart men moved out early. This was high and wild country where winter screamed in out of the north blocking trails, plugging passes, carpeting the primitive back-lands with a foot of snow before Cheyenne over in Wyoming had seen the last autumn leaf fall.

Cattlemen made it a point to complete their high-country gather and be out of the Snake River wilds before the middle of September. Travellers too, rarely lingered in a place where the early winds came scouring with a cold to them that pierced a man's heaviest clothing and chilled him to the bone.

Down at McAllister folks said autumn would be the time for the army to move in, or the U.S. Marshal from over at Boise, because when that exodus began after the first warning wind, that untracked huge Snake River country began to spew forth the desperadoes of every conceivable variety that hid out, back in there.

Sheriff Coffey knew there were wanted men back in there, but Sheriff Coffey had a budget which allowed for the occasional employment of one deputy—providing it was a dire emergency—and for just one day at a time. It wouldn't have made any difference if he'd been permitted to hire a full-time deputy. Those Snake River hills, buttes, breaks, valleys and forests were much too vast for a pair of men to search through in a year, anyway.

Furthermore, the town of McAllister wasn't all that placid and peaceful, that Fred Coffey could go riding out for any length of time. And finally, even in the autumn when they were leaving the high country for warmer places down south, the nightriders ordinarily didn't go out of their way to make trouble. Now and then a horse turned up missing, a shirt disappeared off a clothes line or a chicken failed to appear at the roost at feeding time, but these things could have been the result of depredations committed by migrating Shoshoni redskins or even, for that matter, of an early storm. As Coffey had said more than once, win, lose or draw, there was always a little petty theft anywhere a man

5

went.

What Coffey *didn't* say was that he was relieved each autumn when the high country was empty of men and the worst critter ranchers had to contend with until the following spring was maybe some old rheumatic lobo wolf with half his teeth gone who preyed on weak cattle or young colts.

Those were natural varmints; cattlemen had a sure-fire cure for them. A thirty-thirty bullet between the eyes or a carcass left out enticingly with the paunch liberally laced with strychnine. Anyway, Idaho was a wild, primitive place; no one resided there who expected it to be anything else. Life was a series of encounters; each day brought its particular crisis, if it was nothing more perilous than simply meeting an eight-hundred-pound bear on the trail, a man figured himself fortunate.

Even in the settlements, people were not immune. For one thing everyone went armed, and because armed men came in endless variety, unpredictable things occasionally happened. For another, because Idaho was so primitive, so vast and rugged, so mountainous and untravelled, it was a haven for men who coasted across its borders in the dead of night, wanted by the law in five different states and territories, and sometimes even up in Canada where the Northwest Mounted Police were relentless as far as the international line.

For those who bitterly complained Fred Coffey had a stock answer: 'This is Idaho,' he'd say. 'There aren't two civilized people per square mile for more thousands of square miles than you can wave your hat at. If a man wants higher-priced range, flatter land, more lawmen and higher taxes, he ought to go down to California or back to Missouri.'

There was no getting around the truth of Coffey's statement, either, but at the same time it was the very lack of all those amenities which drew people to Idaho. The trouble was, they were as mottled and tarnished and variegated, even the law-abiding ones, as could be found anywhere on earth just because of the lack of those things, so Fred was tolerant. He probably would've been tolerant anyway, though, for he'd passed fifty a year or two back, and the fires of youth had been banked by the thorough knowledge of age, which said very plainly that no man was going to change the world; only young men tried that and unless they changed, they very often ended up in a shallow grave. The very fact that Fred had reached the half-way mark proved that he was tolerant.

But that only went just so far too; no one committed a felony around McAllister without having to eventually face Coffey, who was a fast man with a gun and a good head to boot. Fred drew a fine line. Only he knew exactly

7

where he drew it, so usually folks were pretty law-abiding. Even the nightriders.

Frank Hall summed it up right well when he said McAllister probably could import a better lawman, but it'd cost a lot more money than Fred was paid, and on top of that, younger lawmen had a habit of stirring up about as much trouble as they ever settled.

Frank owned a horse ranch four miles west of McAllister over near the broken country not far from the Snake River. He'd pioneered the country. It was discreetly rumoured that Frank Hall had come up out of California with a bag full of Wells-Fargo gold. If that were so, then it'd happened at least twenty years earlier, because Frank hadn't been out of Idaho in that length of time, although prior to then he'd disappeared now and then for a month or more at a time.

But regardless of Frank's past, he was now a successful rancher; his horses fetched the highest prices and even army buyers and men from the various Indian agencies around the country journeyed to McAllister to look over Frank Hall's horses.

Frank wasn't a young man; he and Fred Coffey looked to be about the same age- fifty-one or maybe fifty-two. They were built about alike too; lean, leathery, weathered, six feet high and honed down to a hard edge. Fred had more hair than Frank, but to off-set that, Frank was handier with his hands. When he'd been forty-nine he'd waded to his hocks in fighting cowboys at the *Tundall House Saloon* in McAllister, and came through still on his feet, no small feat considering that the men who rode Idaho's cattle ranges were about as rugged a fraternity as could be found anywhere rangeriders congregated.

Peter Pierson who owned the *Tundall House* said afterwards it was the gol-dangdest brawl he'd ever seen in his twenty-five years in the saloon business. Dave Miller the liveryman who happened to also be present that hot summer day, said the same, only Dave, who was younger and brawnier and had gotten into the scrap, added something Pete Pierson couldn't attest to.

'Frank hit me by accident in all the swingin' an' backin', and by gawd I'm here to tell you fellers I been kicked by mares an' horses, burros an' mules, but I never had nothin' to put me down'n out so sudden-like in all my cussed life. Ol' Frank's got a combination o' lead an' dynamite in each hand, believe me about that.'

There was one thing Frank Hall, Fred Coffey, Pete Pierson and Dave Miller had in common: All were bachelors. With Fred and Frank it was a case of not taking any curative steps when they were young enough, and now being past fifty neither cared to change old habits. With Pete and Dave it was a matter of danged few opportunities; Idaho rarely

9

attracted unmarried women. Otherwise, they had their differences of personality, character, and the way they chose to order their lives. As Parson Fleming once said, seeing those four playing poker at Pierson's saloon on the Sabbath, 'The Lord and the Devil just can't decide which one should get them. Neither can I.'

CHAPTER TWO

Agnes Carlisle ran the combination bakery and cafe in McAllister. Until she'd ridden in on the stage one soft spring day three years earlier there'd been a tobacco-chewing old crippled up stage driver who did the cooking and serving, but even the toughest stomachs had been made queasy the way he'd set a man's plate of food down, turn and lustily expectorate on the floor behind his counter, so when Aggie bought him out and spent a week just using lye-water to clean the place up, folks had felt better about eating over there.

It wasn't altogether Aggie's food though; she was a firm-breasted woman with violet eyes, a heavy mouth, and taffy-blonde hair. When she looked into a man's face across her counter, it was as though the sun had just popped out from behind a cloud.

But Agnes Carlisle very soon laid down the

law: She didn't go buggy-riding; she didn't care for box-socials; when she went to one of the rare community dances she went alone, danced with *all* the boys, and she went home alone. In short, Aggie encouraged no one, was friendly with everyone, and had a streak of iron up her back that cooled the most ardent rangerider in a hurry.

Aggie was handsome. She was also very practical. Once, she'd told Fred Coffey that she'd been married; that her husband had died in a gunfight down by Abilene on the Kansas plains. But that was all she said about herself or her past, and Fred had never asked. It was enough just to get a genuine woman-cooked meal. Besides; what possible dark secrets could be lurking in the past of a woman as handsome as Aggie Carlisle?

Frank Hall had once eyed Aggie with sombre thoughts, but in the end he'd done nothing. When a man Frank's age balanced the thing, it didn't make much sense. Except for companionship and good cooking, the drawbacks were many and heavy. But Frank liked to drift in and eat at Aggie's counter nonetheless, and just sort of sip his black coffee and day-dream.

Stocky Dave Miller had been more enterprising; he still had the hungers and the smoulderings of youth. But Aggie had a way of lifting her violet eyes and chilling a man to the bone, so Dave, like Frank, kept coming

11

back for the cooking, but only as a friend.

Aggie liked them all. She told Fred Coffey that one smokey autumn evening when a warm wind was blowing in from the south. 'But I'm not a girl any more, Fred. I'm thirty years old.'

Coffey had gallantly said, 'Thirty on you, Aggie, is like eighteen on the next woman.'

She dazzled Fred with that rare, golden smile of hers. 'If I ever re-marry, I think I'll set my cap for you, Fred.'

They'd had their laugh about that, but Fred blushed all the same. He was old enough to worry a little about her being alone in a raw country, and young enough to carry his shoulders a trifle straighter when he entered the cafe.

But it was in all respects a normal autumn. The men ate at Aggie's cafe, the few women in town such as the harness-maker's wife and the spouse of the general store's paunchy proprietor, and Parson Fleming's mousy little woman, eventually accepted Aggie. They even adopted her into their Civic Betterment League. As Frank Hall told the others that Sunday afternoon he and the others were playing poker when Parson Fleming looked in and caught them at it, 'Another year's about shot, an' we're all still here, no richer, no poorer, no better'n no worse. Are you raising or droppin' out, Pete?'

But that was while the moon was in its first quarter, thin and sharp-edged and pale. It

12

was also while that warm, low wind kept blowing, bringing on an Indian summer where in former years they'd have perhaps had snow, or at least a lot more frost in the mornings then they were now having.

The cowmen were uneasy. Jess Palmer who ran three thousand head east of town said that if this weather kept up it'd keep a decent snow-pack from forming in the mountains, and next spring there'd be floods, while next summer the land would all dry up and blow away.

Jess had a habit of expecting the worst though. His wife'd died the year previous, which had changed him, but he'd never been known for being very jovial anyway. He was a stocky, scarred, iron-hard man in his forties with pale blue eyes and greying hair. He'd worked hard so long building up his holdings that now, when he didn't actually have to, he worked just as hard out of long habit.

It was Jess who rode into McAllister when the moon was in its second quarter to report something out of the ordinary to Fred Coffey over at the jailhouse across from Aggie's cafe. 'You ever hear of fellers ridin' *into* the high country this time o' year, Fred? Well; neither have I, an' I've been around here my share of years. All the same, last night I was out with m'shotgun waitin' for a danged 'coon that's been killin' my hens, and there they went, three of 'em in single file like phantoms, ridin' straight into the hills.'

13

'Rangeriders,' offered Fred. 'Cowboys from some outfit huntin' for stray critters, Jess.'

'At one o'clock in the mornin', Fred, an' ridin' quiet-like as Indians, an' making' a wide path around my buildings, an' with their saddle-guns swung forward, not backwards under their saddle-skirts?'

Fred pondered. As far as he knew there'd been no recent crimes committed close by. At least he'd received no fresh posters on wanted men. Of course that didn't mean a whole lot either, for Idaho's nightriding felons rarely were wanted by Idaho authorities anyway. He temporised. 'Well; as soon as this Indian summer passes an' winter gets down here, they'll pull out quick enough, Jess. I wouldn't worry about it.'

'No,' agreed Jess dourly, 'maybe you wouldn't, Fred. But *I* would. They were on my range; they seen my buildings. I let all my riders go last month. What's to prevent 'em from sneakin' down, when the weather turns bad, an' slittin' my throat in bed?' Palmer put a cold stare upon the sheriff. 'Those three were too close, Fred. Now, I know what goes on in the back country as well as you do, but I'm sayin' those three were too close. And besides; when the storms hit, whose hearth'll they recollect passin' by?'

Coffey turned resigned. 'All right. I'll ride up and have a look around,' he murmured. 'They'll be strangers all right. That's a

14

certainty. This warm weather could end this afternoon an' we could have a foot of snow by sunup tomorrow. In that case, if they weren't too far back in, they'd come out all right, like you say. Otherwise; they'd freeze stiff back in there an' we'd find 'em by the smell next summer.'

Jess was mollified. 'I'll ride with you, if you want, Fred. My work's all finished for the balance of the year anyway.' Coffey agreed to that. He liked company on the trail. 'Fair enough, Jess. I'll be out at your place come sunup. Have the coffee pot on.'

A man's likes and dislikes shape his actions as well as his thoughts. Fred didn't cherish the idea of riding those high-country trails. There was a veritable maze of them, some fresh-made, some as old as the mountains themselves, but they shared one similarity; they all passed back and forth through some of the best drygulching country on earth. If Jess Palmer's three phantoms just happened to be desperate men they not only wouldn't be found, but if they just did happen to be stumbled onto, they could get off the first half dozen shots. It was that kind of country, back there. Of course if it hadn't been, it wouldn't be so popular with the nightriders either.

Fred had supper, as usual, over at Aggie's place. He didn't mention that he was going to ride out; it wasn't *that* important. It was just something he'd rather not have to do, but

15

which he *would* do. Afterwards, he ambled around town making his patrol, then crossed over to the *Tundall House* to see if any of his cronies were around, for a little game of draw-poker.

Pierson wagged his head where he was setting up drinks for a dull gathering, behind his bar. 'Dave got kicked an' went to Doc Heatly's place for an examination,' he told the sheriff when Fred leaned upon his bar. 'I'm too busy tonight anyway for our poker game, Fred. Want a drink?'

Coffey had one; it sat so well he had another one. The crowd was light, but then in the autumn with most of the rangeriders gone, it usually was. A pair of thick-made freighters in plaid wool shirts open half way to their navels were sharing a limp old stale newspaper over near the cold stove. Three old men were playing penny-ante by the north wall. Three rangemen were drinking soberly down the bar, and talking in low, casual tones. Otherwise Pierson's place wasn't very lively tonight.

Fred gave it up after his second drink. According to the clock over the backbar it was nine o'clock. He headed for his room down at the hotel.

The warm wind was still blowing, only now it was higher; up above the town in fact, holding back the advancing cold fronts with a strong persistence. Those hot winds weren't unheard of, but they were rare. So was Indian

16

summer rare; all around, the trees were violent shades of red and yellow and orange, but autumn's customary cold just wasn't able to get through to match the trace of those first few frosts.

At the hotel Fred ran into Carey Holdorf, who owned the general store. Carey was a paunchy, amiable man in his mid-thirties, bald as a badger, and bland. They exchanged a nod and Fred went on up to his room. Whatever Carey was doing at the hotel didn't particularly interest Fred. Carey had one of the best homes in McAllister. He also had a wife who didn't often let Carey out at night for fear he'd fall on evil ways like some of the other men around town had, or at least so she averred, playing poker and drinking down at Pierson's saloon.

Carey was thought to be the wealthiest man in town. There was good reason for folks to credit that suspicion; if he ever went anywhere except from home to the store and back home again, come evening, or if he ever spent a dollar, no one knew about it. A few people envied the Holdorfs because of their affluence, their thriving business and their white-painted house on one of the quieter back roadways, but Aggie Carlisle didn't envy them. In fact, she didn't like Carey's wife very much, and she had her private reasons for strongly disliking paunchy Carey.

He was about the only man around who just didn't take no for an answer. And that,

17

although Fred Coffey didn't know it at the time, or even care one way or another, was precisely what Carey was doing at the hotel that night: Waiting for Agnes to close up her shop and head for the hotel. If Carey's wife had known his thoughts about the time Fred and Carey nodded as the sheriff headed on upstairs to his room, she'd have split Carey's ear and yanked his arm through it.

Doc Heatly came strolling into the hotel moments after Sheriff Coffey had gone upstairs. Doc's first name was George, but no one ever called him by it. He was a very dry, lanky man in his middle thirties, with grey eyes, jet black hair, and a periodic thirst which had made him leave the more settled areas east of the Missouri River four years earlier, to come and settle, and practice, in Idaho. He had a sardonic way of speaking, sometimes caustic, sometimes downright insulting, which kept most folks at arm's distance, but there was no getting around one thing; Doc Heatly was a good physician and surgeon. Or maybe folks just thought he was because there'd never been a doctor in the McAllister country before, except for an army surgeon thirty years before who no one now remembered.

Doc was unquestionably the most learned man around, too. When he saw fat Carey Holdorf fidgeting, glancing at his watch and wearing out the edge of his hat between sweaty hands, he strolled up and said, 'You know,

18

Carey, I can think of perhaps a dozen ways for a man to get into serious trouble, but the most dangerous and intractable way, to my way of thinking, is for a married man like you to make a damned fool of himself over an unmarried woman—like Agnes Carlisle.'

Holdorf got red as a beet. 'You could mind your own business,' he said in a piping voice. 'It *could* be just plain business, you know, Doc.'

Heatly gave his lean, long face a little shake. 'Not when the other person looks like Aggie Carlisle it couldn't, Carey. We both know that. And in case you're really concerned, I just came from her cafe; she's making a big feed for five hungry cattlemen who just arrived in town and won't be locking up until long after midnight tonight.'

Carey's anguish was glaringly apparent. He dropped his hat atop his head, turned and walked out of the hotel, turned right and went treading heavily down the warm night. The moment he turned the far corner, Agnes Carlisle stepped out of shadows and entered the hotel's tiny, threadbare lobby, smiling up at Doc.

'You saved my life,' she said.

'Not your life, only your reputation. Anyway; I was doing Carey an even bigger favour. One of these days his wife's going to catch him watching you.' Doc assumed a sad expression. 'It'll take ten stitches just to close

19

the scalp when she's through with him.'

Aggie's violet eyes twinkled. 'Good night, Doctor, and thanks again.'

Heatly nodded, turned and watched Aggie start up the stairs. There's just no way for a sturdily put together woman to climb stairs demurely. Doc sighed and thought some bitter-sweet thoughts, and turned to leave the hotel. He was over-due up at Pierson's saloon; would in fact have been up there an hour ago except that he'd stopped in for a cup of coffee at Aggie's cafe, and had allowed himself to be talked into ridding the lobby of Carey Holdorf so she could get up to her room without a scene.

He went outside, turned right and started along. Drinking was a terrible vice. It took fifteen years according to medical statistics to become a genuine alcoholic. Doc was thirty-five years old now. In fifteen years he'd be fifty. At fifty a man on the frontier already had one foot in the grave anyway.

CHAPTER THREE

If a man knew under what circumstances he would die, it's a safe bet he'd avoid those circumstances like the plague. Unless of course his occupation was such that he'd already long ago learned to live with both the inevitability of dying and its undeniable connection with what he did for a living.

Fred Coffey had lived with the prospects of sudden and violent death so long that if Doc Heatly or anyone else had told him point-blank the morning he rode out of McAllister bound for Jess Palmer's ranch west and a little south of town that he'd never see another sunrise, he probably wouldn't even have blinked an eye.

But no one told him because no one knew it was true.

Jess Palmer was waiting. He had the coffee hot and a little bait of rolled barley at the barn for Fred's horse. There actually wasn't any great hurry, so far as either Fred or Jess knew. It wasn't as though they were possemen dusting it grimly over the trail of an outlaw. All they had to be concerned with after they rode out, was that they'd arrive back at Jess's place before nightfall.

They had their coffee, talked a little, speculating on which trails the riders might have taken in the back-country, and considered it probable that they'd never see them anyway, unless both they and their horses had been bushed, simply because they'd let a lot of time go by since Jess had spied the strangers.

Still, when they rode out of Palmer's yard Jess had a little pouch of jerky, and they both were well armed. For the first few miles Fred

21

knew the country well enough, but after that Jess took over; he'd been chousing cattle out of this country a lot longer than he'd like to have recalled. Where Fred only knew it in a general way, Jess knew it intimately.

It turned warmer as the sun climbed. Both men shed their jumpers and Jess ruefully shook his head, returning to his earlier complaints about his cussed un-naturally hot autumn weather laying in a lot of grief for them all come next summer. Fred didn't comment. They'd picked up the tracks of three shod horses a mile back, perfectly embedded in the rank dust of an old cow trail. 'If they didn't branch off it,' Coffey said, pointing downward at the tracks, 'we ought to eventually see them.'

'No place to get off this particular trail,' explained Jess, eyeing the rising breaks and slopes around them. 'It heads straight back into a dead-end canyon where a little creek comes out of the sidehill. I've camped there many times, out huntin' cattle in the autumn.'

They passed from brilliant sunlight down into the gloomy depths of the canyon, and Fred understood why Jess had said those three strangers couldn't get off this particular trail.

There were some scabby old junipers struggling to keep alive in shale-rock soil no more than eight inches deep. Otherwise the vegetation was mostly buck-brush, sage, chaparral, scrub oak and the like, with now

22

and then a streak of red-barked pines standing up like thinned-out hair atop the domes and down the craggy sidehills. It was a rugged, raw, inhospitable country with three natural attributes: water, grass, and solitude.

Deer sign was plentiful. So was bear and elk sign. Grouse and valley quail pecked at the grass seed, and of course, as Jess Palmer had often pointed out, the cattle that turned up missing each fall hadn't fallen off any cliffs nor been eaten by bears and lobos; they'd been shot, skinned out, fried, roasted, and jerked, by two-legged predators.

Fred came across the remains of an old campfire in a gloomy place with the canyon walls pushed back on either side making enough room for a camp and a little pasture for three animals. He and Jess explored the tracks. They matched perfectly with the same tracks they'd followed this far, so they pushed on. It wasn't quite noon when they left that spot, so the overhead sunshine couldn't as yet reach down into their grey-layered brushy canyon. They probably should've been more careful; the site and the circumstances were ideal for an ambush, except that they expected none, weren't actually manhunting, and since the back-country was emptied of outlaws this time of year, were relying on habit and custom more than wariness and suspicion.

The trail began to widen out a little, a mile beyond that dead campsite. The hills sloped away and more underbrush appeared; there were even a few stately old giant pines and firs, and eventually the tail-race of that onward creek Jess had spoken of, appeared at the side of the trail, now and then showing the darting, squirming shadows of trout-minnows.

Fred was on ahead, eyeing the slopes, keeping watch for that dead-end Jess had spoken of. The trail alternated between rattling shale and muffling dust, but in a place like this where cliff faces occasionally appeared to heighten acoustics, sounds travelled a long way up and down the canyon.

Fred hauled down to an abrupt halt. Jess nearly piled into him from behind. 'What is it?' Palmer asked sharply, and Fred pointed up ahead. There were three tucked-up horses standing in a little two or three acre meadow which was closed off on three sides. They were eating tall grass. There were the unmistakable marks of hard-riding and sweat on each animal.

Jess studied the animals, the cul-de-sac itself, and eased his horse up beside Fred Coffey to crane around for some sign of the men who owned those animals up there. He said something about going the rest of the way on foot; was bending down to dismount, when a crashing volley of gunfire erupted from both slopes, on their right and on their left. Jess's hat sailed away. He reacted to being ambushed like this with lifelong

24

instinctiveness. He dropped like a stone and began to roll towards the side of the trail where that little creek had cut deeply into the rock. There was brush over there, even a few sapling trees. He got into cover before he had time to look for Fred Coffey.

The sheriff was still atop his saddle, bending lower each time the excited animal turned and shied. Without a sound he pitched headlong to the ground, finally, as his mount gave a quick little sidewards crow-hop. He landed hard and loose. Jess stared. Coffey made no move to catch hold of his animal's reins nor to reach down for his belt-gun. In fact, he didn't move at all after he fell in the dust.

Jess lifted his eyes and raked them along the opposite slope, but he didn't see man or movement. He lay there scarcely breathing while his horse and Coffey's animal turned and started back down the canyon, taking with them both those carbines in the saddle-scabbards. Jess ground his teeth about that. All he had was his sixgun; for a prolonged battle at long range it was about as useless as a third leg on a man.

The sun finally crept above the highest rim and poured good light down into the canyon. Silence grew and piled up. Somewhere, three gunmen were crouching, waiting to get a glimpse of Palmer, and he knew it. The only way out was the same way he'd come to this place. If he stayed close and was lucky, he

25

might be able to crawl through the creekside underbrush and perhaps at least get beyond rifle range, but it was doubtful.

Still, the alternative was to lie there like a sitting duck until those invisible killers inched carefully around behind where they could see him. Then he'd get the same dose Fred had gotten.

Jess dashed sweat off his forehead and peered out at Sheriff Coffey. He was lying exactly where he'd landed; he hadn't moved. There was no question about it, Fred had either been killed, or he was hard hit and unconscious. Jess raised his eyes to scan the slopes again. If he could get out there maybe Fred would only be bleeding. Perhaps he could save him or at least make him easy before he cashed in.

He decided to try palavering. It was either that, or try sneaking away. If he got clear he'd have to abandon the sheriff. He had no doubt at all but that this would be the same as condemning Fred to death. The trouble was, if he sang out now, those patient killers out there would know where he was hiding from his voice. Two dead men up here weren't going to be a help to anyone. Jess was torn by indecision, but he never had to make that judgement, it was made for him.

Up the south slope a carbine erupted, its whiplash sound bouncing off the hillsides roundabout. Dust burst to life beside Fred

Coffey. He didn't move. Jess waited to pick up the tell-tale dirty smoke from that gunshot. When it drifted over the spiny top of a flourishing big clump of sage Jess swung his pistol to bear. But the range was too great for a gun whose barrel was only six inches long. He cursed under his breath and gritted his teeth.

From up the westerly slope off to Jess's right a man's booming, hoarse voice sang out. 'That one's dead, Slim. Where'd the other one get to?'

Slim called back from a different spot than where he'd dumped that shot downwards towards Fred Coffey, but that was all Jess could determine because the canyon tossed his answer back and forth so it could've come from almost anywhere.

'How d'you know that one's dead?'

'Because,' came back the man up there in the rocks on Jess's right, 'I saw his shirt puff dust when the slug hit him right over the heart. Now where's that other one?'

'I think he ducked up towards the horses along the creek,' Slim answered.

That was wrong; Jess had ducked eastward, which was away from their horses up in the cul-de-sac. His heart began to beat with renewed hope. He turned, quickly scanned the lower route out of the canyon in the direction their saddled horses had fled, and licked dry lips. He could make it if he took lots of time and moved very carefully; there was enough heavy undergrowth along the creek-bank to shicld him for a long way.

He put up his pistol, turned and began crawling on all fours. Fred Coffey was dead. There was no reason for Jess to remain in this place. What he had to somehow do now, was get out of this lethal canyon, catch his horse, and ride like the devil was after him, for McAllister.

As he crawled he wished the sun hadn't come over the rimrocks, but it had, so he had to be very careful. He'd gotten nearly a hundred yards away when he heard those men back in there calling back and forth again. They sounded annoyed and anxious now. He couldn't distinguish their words but he could guess their thoughts. They had to find Jess and do it fast, then kill him, otherwise, if he got out of this place he'd unquestionably return with a posse. Killing lawmen, even in wild and untamed Idaho, was about the worst crime men could commit.

Sweat drove him down to the creek once for a drink of cold water. It made him feel better; it also made him feel hotter. After that he took risks. He dashed across several wide clearings and once, instead of staying low and skirting a shale-rock landslide, he scrambled right up and over it and down the far side, because that was the most direct route.

The sun was over his left shoulder before he felt secure enough to ease out onto the trail peering downward where the horses had gone. They could, of course, run all the way back down to open country, but that was unlikely. Horses were giddy things when they were frightened, but they lacked the ability to concentrate for long, so after they'd run and became winded, they ordinarily halted, gauged their surroundings, and if nothing occurred to further frighten them, they reverted to their habitual preoccupation with their bellies: Food took over invariably where fright left off.

They were down there, a hundred or so yards ahead where that earlier wide place in the trail had initially halted Jess and Fred near the dead campsite, grazing with their reins dragging. Jess knew his mount very well; he could only walk up to it if the animal were convinced it couldn't run away from him. He had to slip around it then.

Those killers back there would find out soon enough that he hadn't crawled back up towards their cul-de-sac, but had instead escaped eastward. They'd be after him with carbines very soon now, if they weren't already after him. He started down towards the horses.

Where the trail widened he had to get out into the creek to get around the grazing , animals. The water was cold; it stung him to an anxiety he had to fight hard to control. If he let the horses hear or see him, they'd leave him

29

afoot. He'd never escape from three mounted killers on foot. He stopped once to calm himself, then continued on all fours down the creek where he made not a sound.

It worked. He got around the horses. Where a little bare spot appeared he came through it back up onto the trail. At once both horses saw him and threw up their heads. He forced himself to walk very slowly and casually forward, speaking soothingly as he went. His animal fidgeted, looking around. It could retreat back up the canyon by the dusty trail but that was its only way clear. He desperately talked and held out a hand, always advancing. Fred Coffey's animal dropped its head and plucked a mouthful of grass. Jess concentrated on this beast, which seemed calm and able to be caught. He got up to it, reached out very carefully, grabbed the reins at the precise moment his own horse whirled and bolted back up the trail. Fred's critter would have jerked free and followed after but Jess held on for dear life.

He talked himself on up, put a hand upon the horse's neck, calmed it, then stepped around, toed in and sprang up to settle across the dead man's saddle. Somewhere back up the canyon he heard a man's ringing shout echo back and forth among the sidehills. Undoubtedly, the gunmen had seen Jess's animal running back up towards them. Jess didn't waste a moment; he could tell by those shouts that his enemies were mounted and pushing on down towards him. He set Fred Coffey's horse to the trail in a rapid lope and held the horse to it until the canyon's twists and turns debouched out upon the lower-down plains. There, he briefly halted scanning the back country, then pointed the horse towards McAllister and hooked it hard with both spurs.

It was nearly three o'clock in the afternoon by then. Before he saw McAllister hull-down on the far horizon, it was close to dusk.

CHAPTER FOUR

Dave Miller was limping around his liverybarn with the aid of a cane when Jess Palmer rode in. Jess called over to him that Fred Coffey was dead. Dave stopped and looked stunned, leaving Jess to dismount and put up the sheriff's horse unaided.

'Where?' Dave finally gasped. 'How?'

'Back in the hills northwest o' my range,' replied Palmer. 'I got to go get a drink. Round up some fellers an' meet me up at Pierson's saloon.'

What Jess really needed was food, but it didn't occur to him. When he walked into the *Tundall House*, Pete was throwing dice with Frank Hall and Doc Heatly for the drinks.

31

Jess burst upon them the same way he had upon Dave Miller.

'Fred Coffey's dead back in the damned mountains,' he said loudly, striking the bartop with a balled-up fist. 'Pete; give me a double shot of rye whiskey!'

There were a number of townsmen in Pierson's saloon, some drinking, some idly conversing, some playing cards with the few cowmen scattered throughout the room. Every head came up, every set of eyes jumped over to linger on Jess Palmer.

Pete filled the water-glass with Jess's double shot and leaned on the bar watching Palmer down it neat. 'What happened?' he afterwards asked. Pete made a motion for the glass to be re-filled. Water brimmed up into his eyes; that whiskey was as green as a new hide.

'I saw some nightriders yesterday. Fred come out to my place this morning. We went trailin' em'. They ambushed us back in a dead-end canyon. We didn't get no warnin' at all. One minute we was ridin' up the trail. The next minute they cut loose. I was half down the side o' my horse fixin' to dismount. Even then, one of the bullets took off my hat. But Fred caught one head on. He sat up there for a few seconds, then dropped like a busted doll right out of his saddle.' Jess downed the second double shot, made a frightful grimace and pushed the glass away with one hand while he dragged a soiled sleeve across his teary eyes

32

with the other hand. 'I got away because they went lookin' for me where I wasn't.'

Frank Hall was a long-time friend of Fred Coffey. He straightened up slowly off the bar and looked around at the other ranchers in the saloon. 'No sense in waitin',' he exclaimed. 'They'll be headin' deeper into the badlands as it is. Let's go.' As chairs scraped backwards and men stood up, Frank said, 'Jess; get a fresh animal from Dave Miller and show us where it happened.'

A number of townsmen began clamouring to go along. No one discouraged them; no one bothered as everyone, even Pete Pierson, started for the roadway door and out into the star-washed night. Pete had a relief-man he sometimes used at the bar. Now, he swerved away and went loping towards that man's shack. As he ran along he yanked off his bar-room apron.

Dave Miller was limping up the middle of the roadway in the weak light with four other men. They met Frank Hall's contingent about in front of Dave's livery-barn. Before Dave could volunteer the information that the men with him had volunteered to ride, Frank said, 'No sense in a big mob of us goin'. Just the fellers who're used to hardship on horseback. The badlands are damned rough; no dudes or clerks better come along. The rest of you fetch your horses and guns and get back here to Dave's barn as fast as you can.'

Doc Heatly was far back in the van of the men from Pierson's saloon. Now he walked on up by Frank, where most of the men were beginning to walk away, and said, 'Frank; hadn't we better do some calm thinking first?'

Hall turned his rugged old seamed, weathered face. Starshine shown off it like blue steel. 'What is there to think about, Doc? You heard Jess: Three nightriders dry-gulched Fred. That's all we need to know, except where it happened an' what trail they took after killing him.'

'But hell, Frank; by the time we get out there it'll be too dark to trail them.'

'It won't be too dark to get a right good start at sunup,' snapped Hall, and put a hard look over at Heatly.

'Maybe you'd better stay here in town, Doc. This won't be anything you're used to.'

Heatly gave Hall his hard look right back, and quietly said, 'The riding, Frank, or the lynching; which do you mean I won't be used to?'

Hall didn't answer. He turned his back on Doc Heatly and said, 'Jess; dammit all, don't be standin' around. Go fetch a fresh horse.'

Palmer was feeling much better now. 'Dave's bringing me a fresh horse,' he answered with spirit. 'What're *you* waitin' for?'

Frank turned on his heel and headed over to the tie-rack in front of Pierson's saloon where other rangemen were already getting astride. Someone over there called from the saddle to a man upon the sidewalk, asking him to ride out and explain to the mounted man's wife where he'd gone and why he wouldn't be home tonight.

The town gradually began to congregate as the word of Fred Coffey's murder was called swiftly from house to house. Even Agnes Carlisle, her long hair caught up hastily and knotted to fall down between her shoulders, appeared over in the hotel doorway. Men and women came walking along from sideroads, most of the men with arms, most of the women excited and hastily dressed.

By the time a large crowd had collected the possemen were mounted and ready. By then too, Jess's load of rye whiskey was turning him loud and agitated. He gestured at the horsemen calling profanely upon them to get organized, to follow him.

The last man to leave McAllister was the last man to go to his buggy shed, rig out a saddle animal and fling himself into the saddle: Doc Heatly. The others were already turning a far corner northward, jerking roadway dust to life under their hooves, as Doc came out into the roadway. He saw the riders and spurred after them. A woman called out as Doc loped by. He didn't look around but he waved backwards and kept right on riding.

There were nine of them, counting Doc.

Frank Hall and Jess Palmer were out ahead. The others were equally divided between townsmen and cattlemen, but the guns they carried were identical: Colt six's and Winchester thirty-thirties. The cattlemen also had hardtwist catch-ropes coiled at their saddle-swells, but none of them had much more and several of the townsmen had forgotten to fetch along coats. Not that they needed them now, but this was Indian summer; it could end almighty sudden, as Fred Coffey had observed only the day before.

Frank kept the lead as far as Palmer's ranch. After that Jess took over. Two hours later, as they were pushing right along towards the mouth of that fatal canyon, Jess began to turn quiet. His whiskey was wearing off somewhat. When a rider flashed a match to light a cigarette Jess swore at him.

'They could still be in here. What you fixin' to do; get us all ambushed?'

Frank thought differently but said only a few soothing words to calm the prickled sensibilities of the man Jess had cursed. 'I know this canyon, boys; if they were at the far end of it before, they sure won't be there now. It's a dead-end. They'd figure a posse would be after them. No one in his right mind'd let a posse catch him in a dead-end canyon.'

Hall was right. When they came to the place where the fight had erupted, Fred Coffey was still lying exactly where he'd fallen. He was as

36

stiff as a ramrod too. Beyond, where Jess went ahead afoot, crouched over and with a carbine, those three horses were no longer grazing, and even in the poor light it was obvious that those nightriders had struck their camp in a big hurry, before leaving.

When Jess read all the sign he could make out in the darkness and went back, the others had Fred tied across a horse. Doc Heatly was saying: 'Three inches above the heart. Jess: you say he didn't drop right away?'

'No, Doc; he sat up there for a few seconds, then commenced to droop down, an' finally he fell. Why?'

'Well; he was dead within seconds after that bullet hit him. Only a powerful will could have kept a man upright even a couple of seconds after that slug hit him. It severed the aorta. I'll perform an autopsy after we get back, but I'm sure that's what happened.'

Jess spoke harshly. 'That doesn't matter, Doc. What matters is that Fred's dead.'

The others murmured assent with Jess's statement. Frank Hall stood long and lean and stonily silent, gazing over at the dead man being securely fastened across leather. 'Somebody ride back with the body,' he said, eventually. 'Lay him out in the backroom of Holdorf's store until we can all get back an' give Fred a proper send-off.'

The man who owned the horse Coffey was tied upon, nodded his head and permitted two

37

cowmen give him a hand up behind the cantle. He was one of the townsmen. A man named Jack Spencer who worked as a freight-rig swamper occasionally. As the others moved aside Spencer reined his horse back down the trail through a dark wall of total silence.

When Spencer passed around a bend, Frank Hall let his breath out, gazed around, then reached for the reins to his mount. 'Might as well give the horses a rest up there in the grass,' he said, starting forward towards the place where the canyon widened and ended in that cul-de-sac. 'Nothin' more to do now until sunup.'

They trooped silently on up into the little meadow, murmuring among themselves, making smokes which it was safe to light now, or so they thought, and loosening their cinchas so the horses could move off better.

Jess made another scout all around. Frank and Doc sat down like Indians around the dead coals of the campfire the nightriders had abandoned. Doc had a bottle. He passed it around. Most of the men took a long pull, but one or two abstained. They weren't the cattlemen.

When Jess came back, dropped down upon his heels and leaned upon his carbine to accept the bottle from Doc and take a drink, he afterwards said, 'They had to go nearly all the way back before they could cut up out of this danged canyon and head overland again.

Maybe a couple of us ought to ride out an' sniff around.'

'Why?' asked Frank Hall. 'So's they can hear you an' get you good like they got Fred, this time? We'll stay right here until sunup, Jess.'

Pete Pierson strolled up and dropped something in front of Frank. It was a worn-out old grey blanket with holes in it. The others strolled on up to stand around Hall and Doc and Jess, watching as Heatly picked up the blanket and flipped it out. Frank suddenly bent over the portion of the ragged hem where it had landed directly in front of him.

'Montana State Penitentiary,' he read aloud.

The others dropped down and crowded in to jostle each other as they also made out that stencilled wording on the blanket. It was difficult to make out because the starlight was weak, but also because the blanket was badly worn. Nonetheless, that's what it said, without any question. *Montana State Penitentiary*.

The only one this legend meant anything to was Jess Palmer, he reared back and looked around. 'Well hell,' he exclaimed. 'When I first saw those three they were ridin' up this way from the south. That's what I told Fred before we came up here. We figured they were from down-country, maybe. But this changes things. They were from up north—from Montana. That means they were headin' south, actually.'

Hall concurred. 'Sure; probably saw McAllister, saw the mountains, and figured to hole-up for a while and maybe drift down into town when it looked safe to do so.'

Heatly didn't accept this sudden assessment. He said, 'Anyone could've owned this blanket. Look at it; the thing's old and worn out. Probably the man who was originally given the blanket traded it off or sold it or maybe it was even stolen from him. This thing doesn't prove they're ex-convicts.'

'No one said it did, Doc,' stated Frank Hall. 'But it'll satisfy me about them, until we catch up an' get the real story from those damned bushwhackers firsthand.'

Jess nodded. So did the others. Doc subsided, reached for his bottle, squinted to see what was left in it, which wasn't very much, tipped back his head and drained the thing. He then tossed it over into the underbrush near the creek.

Jess watched Pete Pierson fold the blanket. 'I'll tell you one thing about the man who left that thing behind,' he muttered. 'He's a lousy murderer. They didn't give us a chance. We weren't out to hunt them down exactly; we just wanted to get a look at them, is all.'

'You got it,' said Doc, delving into a coat pocket for his handkerchief. 'What were you two doing, pokin' along up in here on the trail of three nightriders—not looking where you were going?'

Jess reddened in the darkness and glared at Doc, but never answered. It was true; there was no denying that he and Coffey had acted like a pair of novices. Had gotten themselves ambushed like greenhorns. Even the townsmen dropped their eyes from Jess's flushed countenance and painstakingly studied the ground. The cattlemen, whose lifetime environment was attuned to this kind of violence, deliberately became busy making smokes, or strolled over to check their mounts.

Fred Coffey was the friend of every man there, yet they didn't make any excuses for his carelessness, especially since he'd been a lifelong peace officer. They only shook their heads mutely over old Fred's last mistake, and thought ahead to exacting vengeance. They didn't have to excuse Fred anyway; all they had to be concerned with was his murder; careless or not, Fred had died by ambush. There could be no mitigating circumstances.

They eventually lay back to scan the heavens or smoke, or to catch forty winks before dawn arrived again. All talk ceased and the long night ran on. Doc Heatly and Frank Hall were the last pair to close their eyes. One was adamant, one was resigned.

CHAPTER FIVE

When Jess led them back out of the dead-end canyon the sun was still several hours from rising, but the heavens were steely-grey, so they could at least see around.

There were eight of them, and those two or three who'd overlooked bringing along jumpers or sweaters shivered a little because even with that high warm-front up above, the pre-dawns were still cooler than any other time of day.

Jess proved himself a competent tracker, but then he knew the ground they were passing over. Where the first game-trail veered up a sidehill he dismounted, walked over and got down on one knee seeking sign. There was none; at least there was no sign of shod horses. They rode on to the next trail leading upwards. That time Jess triumphantly pointed up where the sidehill drifted slopingly upwards towards a wind-scoured top-out. They had gone up out of the canyon by this trail.

It required a half hour to get up there where the land lay flat for a fair distance all around before rising up again toward some craggy old barren stone rimrocks. They held a little council as they poked along, and meanwhile the sun began to boost golden shafts from down the far side of the world up into the steely sky.

The tracks were fresh. They were also hurrying. Jess and several of the others pointed that out. A shod horse in a hurry landed flat-down the same as a walking horse, but when he turned his ankle up to move out again, the toe of his shoe dug in hard and deep even in summer-hard ground.

Frank Hall made a smoke for breakfast and scanned the roundabout peaks and slopes. 'They're probably up there somewhere right now, spyin' on us,' he told Doc. 'That's what's wrong with trailin' men in hilly country. All they got to do to see you is get higher'n you are.'

One of the townsmen's mounts twisted an ankle sliding down a rocky hillside and the man had to profanely turn back. That left seven of them still going.

The trail was straight as an arrow for two miles, then went down into a rocky canyon, turned northward and went angling along through the junipers and rocks and buck-brush until it heaved up over the far rim and hit flat going again. Pierson said at the rate they were going—both the men from McAllister and the bushwhackers—their pace would have to set some kind of a record for slowness, and he was correct. The only place the possemen, or the nightriders either for that matter, could make any time at all, was when

43

they encountered those relatively flat places. Even then, though, when the others might have pushed on, Frank and Jess forbade it.

'They got a long lead,' Frank explained. 'All they need is for our horses to give out. If anyone does any runnin' let them do it.'

At high noon they were still riding up and down the slopes passing constantly deeper into more rugged, wild country. The heat was good for a while, then it became tedious. They stopped as often as was necessary to tank up on creek water and to let their animals sip. They had no grub with them.

In one place the men they were after had halted to have a smoke and rest their animals. The brown-paper cigarette butts were lying where they'd been stamped out. Horse tracks were plentiful there too. Doc turned and gazed back the way the possemen had come. 'If they were at this spot an hour or so ago,' he stated, 'they saw us coming. If they stopped here perhaps about sunup, they wouldn't have seen us because we were just climbing up out of the canyon.'

Frank Hall was sardonic. 'Good figurin', Doc,' he said. 'But for one thing. You're lookin' in the wrong direction. They'll be watchin' up ahead of where we are now.'

Frank was right, too.

Up ahead the land got steeper and wilder. There were huge rock formations where nothing grew except an occasional stunted little scraggly clump of brush in some crevice. They saw eagles when they passed around a narrow ledge, and straight below them, a churning creek boiling through some granite narrows. Behind those narrows the water had spread out making a small clear water lake. The ledge they used was part of some ancient trail which hung out in places dangerously close to sudden drop-offs. Here, two of the townsmen found a wide place, dismounted unashamedly, and led their animals. They had reason; one mis-step in this place and the men would fall to their deaths far below where jagged rocks lay in tumbled disarray.

Frank and Jess knew both this trail and the country beyond. They said there were only a few miles of this narrow, sheer travelling, and after that the riders would be out upon a wide rim. It proved true; they left the eagle-infested canyon, went over a cedar-lined hump, and ahead stood the high, wind-scoured rim. Here, they halted again. Jess pointed far ahead where shadows were forming.

'There's a ranch up yonder,' he said, but the others couldn't make out any buildings, and one townsman wanted to know who, in tarnation, would live in a place like this where he had to fetch everything in by crossing the shale-rock trail behind them. Jess smiled and glanced at Frank Hall. 'That's not the only trail in here,' he explained. 'But you're forgettin' somethin'. We're not tryin' to get anywhere, boys. We're trailin' three men. *They* picked this route, we didn't.'

They went on, Jess and Frank riding side by side when the trail was wide enough, conversing occasionally and glancing on ahead where they could leave the rim and descend towards the green parks and pine-lined byways down below. They seemed to know this place well. Doc told Pete Pierson unless a man was an outlaw himself he couldn't imagine him living in such a wild and isolated spot. Pierson agreed.

They were miles from that ranch. When they eventually came close enough to make out buildings, they were curious all over again. Someone, with painstaking care and prodigious labour, had peeled every log, notched and squared every corner, and reinforced every ridge. There was a large barn, a long, low log house set in among some shielding pines, and even some outbuildings, all erected with a lot of thought and sweat.

One of the cattlemen, who operated east of McAllister, said he'd never been back this far into the high country before. That brought a dry rejoinder from Doc Heatly.

'You probably never had any reason. I'd say few *honest* men would have occasion to hide out this far from everything and everybody.'

Jess and Frank exchanged a look, but neither spoke nor even changed expression. They didn't say anything even when a

46

hard-stabbing flash of dazzling brilliance sprang from a hilltop not far from the buildings, obviously some kind of a signal.

One of the townsmen piped up excitedly to draw everyone's attention to that heliograph sign. The men spoke up sharply, confident that one of the killers they were trailing had seen the riders coming and had flashed a warning to his friends.

Frank finally said, when the talk was at its heated height, 'If it's the bushwhackers I'll bet you they sure earned it when they took over that piece of shiny steel.' He and Jess exchanged another look, but this time each of them ruefully grinned. 'Boys,' Frank explained. 'The feller who lives up there has been usin' those old army steel mirrors to signal down to his house that strangers were coming ever since I can remember. He's an old trapper and hunter. Used to battle redskins right here in this place. In fact his woman was a Ute. She's been dead for about ten years now. There's just old Jason and his girl.'

'And,' said a townsman, 'the outlaws. They sure wouldn't pass a place like this, especially if this old duffer's got grub and fresh horses.'

'He's got both,' confirmed Jess. 'But I'll tell you something. If Jason didn't want to give 'em up I wouldn't want to be the feller to try and take 'em away from him.'

The others fell silent as Frank and Jess led

them straight up a long clearing where horses and cattle were standing among the trees on either side, drowsily wagging their tails and eyeing the strangers. Dead ahead lay the weathered, sturdy buildings. There were a pair of wagon ruts leading away from the ranchyard easterly through the trees. They evidently junctured with the north-south stageroad somewhere well along through the rough country, but from where the riders were advancing there was only a flash now and then of that old wagonroad, where the trees were thin and the shadows hadn't yet obscured the sun.

No one spoke. They were within a couple hundred yards of the buildings, still with Jess and Frank leading, but the atmosphere seemed hushed and brooding and too still and quiet; it was almost as though anything which was said this close to the buildings might be heard by someone unfriendly to outlanders. Pete Pierson did mutter something just before they reached the open gate leading on into the orchard and beyond, into the yard. He asked if this old feller who lived up in here like a hermit didn't have anything to do but sit on that blasted little hill up back of his house watching for strange riders.

Frank shrugged, nearly smiling. 'I'd guess it wasn't Jason who spotted us and signalled. I'd guess it was Jess, his daughter. They both pack those little steel army mirrors. As

48

for sittin' up there watchin'. I got a right sound idea whichever one was up there had a darned good reason. There've been other riders through here ahead of us.'

'No,' moaned Pierson. 'That'll mean they got fresh horses.'

Jess wasn't so sure of that. 'Not necessarily, boys. Not necessarily. They didn't get any unless Jason wanted them to have them.'

They passed through an orchard where the leaves were a silent explosion of vivid colours, reached the next open gate and passed on into the yard. A big strapping man stepped forth from the barn with a shotgun up in both hands, and a streaked beard that hung half way to his waist. He was massive and black-eyed and as oaken as men ever came. If any of the other riders besides Jess and Frank had expected some rickety anachronism from the oldtime Indian-fighting past, they were rudely shocked, for although that thick-thewed, mighty man up ahead with the shotgun was certainly in his fifties, he was about as far from being rickety as anyone they'd ever seen. In fact the shotgun he was holding looked almost like a toy weapon in his huge hands.

Jess raised his right hand and sang out. 'Howdy, Jason. It's Palmer and Frank Hall, along with some other fellers from down McAllister way.'

49

The shotgun dropped away but the wide-legged, challenging stance didn't alter one whit as the riders came on up in a slow walk, hauled down to a stop and sat their saddles trading looks with the bearded man.

'Boys,' said Jess to the possemen, 'this here is Jason Weatherell. Jason; these are friends of mine and Frank's. We're trackin' three nightriders who shot down Fred Coffey yesterday and killed him.'

Jason eyed the possemen, his black eyes making a slow, deliberate, circuit as though he intended to memorise each face. Then he gravely nodded, leaned on his scattergun and squinted up at Frank Hall.

'They were here,' he said. 'Frank; you aimin' on hangin' 'em?'

Hall didn't answer right away. There was some byplay between Jason Weatherell and Frank. The latter sat his saddle returning massive Jason's look from an expressionless face. There was no sense of hostility, no electricity in the air around them, but there definitely was something very indelibly different between them. Then Frank offered his answer slowly and sternly.

'What would you recommend, Jason? They shot Fred down like he was a sheep-killin' dog or a calf-killin' wolf. You recommend mercy for that type, Jason?'

'I don't have to recommend it, Frank. The Lord's will be done. Vengeance is mine, saith

50

the Lord; I shall repay. That's right clear, isn't it, Frank?'

'It's clear, Jason, and these men with me today are the Lord's tools for repayin', too.'

Weatherell ran a slow look from face to face among the tired, hungry, rumpled riders. 'Look more like a bunch of dog-tired horsemen to me,' he murmured, then raised his jet-black gaze to Hall again, let it linger briefly, then drifted it on over to Jess Palmer as he said, 'You too, Jess; you want to strangle those men.'

'Those nightriders y'mean,' retorted Jess. 'Jason; they didn't give Fred a chance. I was right there. They tried to bushwhack me too.'

'They were running for their lives, Jess. A man in mortal terror don't figure like you'n I do.'

'That's the gospel truth,' exclaimed Jess, giving his head a hard downward tug. 'But I never murdered anyone yet either, an' I've been in a bad spot or two in my lifetime.'

Frank Hall loosened where he sat. 'Jason,' he said. 'We need some food, a couple of coats if you can spare 'em, and fresh horses.'

Jason brought that ebony glance of his back to Frank again. 'To help you commit murder?' he asked, then gravely shook his head from side to side.

Several of the possemen murmured. One of them, a townsman with a peeling, sunburned nose, said, 'Mister; if it's the principle o' the

51

thing you're fretting about—why just you stay right here an' we'll do the dirty work.'

Jason gazed at that posseman a long time before he said, 'Son; evil begets evil. Wickedness brings on more wickedness. Fred Coffey is dead. The strangled murderers can't change that. But if you lynch those men without a decent trial before God and man, you'll be steeped in their evil the same as though you'd killed Fred Coffey yourself. Mark my word, boy; vengeance is not yours to exact!'

The townsman leaned back in his saddle, blinked, then turned and looked in bewildered amazement around at his companions. They were staring in an uncomprehending way at that massive, bearded patriarch standing there blackly glaring at them.

CHAPTER SIX

'Well,' Frank told them as Jason Weatherell turned to go inside his barn and speak to someone over there, 'now you know about the feller you were all so quick to say had to be hidin' from the law to live so far away from everything.'

That townsman to whom old Jason had spoken sniffed. 'He's one of those religious characters; one of those holier-than-thou fellers. Frank; what's to keep us from just takin' the horses. There are seven o' us.'

'No,' stated Jess with a bitter shake of his head. 'I run cattle up in here. So does Frank run his horses up here when the feed's good. Jason's kind of odd, but I've heard enough about him back a few years to tell you we're not goin' to force him to do anything. He's one of the last fellers around I want for an enemy.'

Another townsman glared barnward and said harshly, 'Then we might as well give up an' turn back, Jess. Our horses are tuckered an' I'll give you odds that old whiskery cuss give fresh mounts to the nightriders.'

Doc Heatly turned and strolled away from the men standing by their horses out there, heading for the barn. The others were too busy arguing to miss him until he emerged from the barn with old Jason and a girl whose appearance startled all of them, except Jess and Frank.

She was tall; perhaps five feet seven or eight, and full breasted and small waisted. Her hair was long and as black as the inside of a well. But her eyes were a bright shade of green, and her features were patrician although her skin was a smooth golden colour.

She was Jason's child, there was no disputing that; she had his same forthright gaze, the same rounded, full jaw and square chin, and undoubtedly at one time Jason's hair had been as midnight-black as her hair was.

The men gazed at her while those three walked on over to them from the barn. Doc's mouth was pulled down a little in a saturnine quirk. He knew men; he knew exactly what those six men over there including old Jess and Frank Hall, were thinking. It was the natural turn of mind for any healthy men who first saw anything as alluringly handsome as Jessica Weatherell.

Jason said, his deep-down voice rumbling out at them, 'This is my daughter, Jessica, boys. She was ridin' the back country and saw you fellers comin' around the south bluffs.'

Jess touched his hatbrim and smiled. The beautiful girl smiled gravely at both Jess and Frank, whom she obviously was already acquainted with. For the men she didn't know she had a little, curt nod. Jason spoke again.

'She was followin' the three strangers when she saw you fellers comin' and signalled me, then turned back.'

Frank Hall nodded. 'Tell me this,' he said to Jason. 'Did they get fresh horses here?'

Jason shook his head. 'They asked; they even offered new-minted gold. But I've had a policy for many years. I don't sell horses to nightriders.'

Pete Pierson scratched his head. 'There were three of them,' he said, as though he doubted Jason. 'And there's just one of you, Mister Weatherell. They're killers. Couldn't they have ridden out into your pasture and roped themselves three fresh animals?'

Jessica said, 'This isn't the first time men like that have come here. No one sneaks up on us. We knew they were coming an hour before they got here. It doesn't matter how we knew. I rode out, pushed the horses clear, then went up onto the hill and kept watch. There were no horses when they got here.'

Jason smiled through his beard. 'But there was my shotgun,' he added. 'No sir, boys; they didn't get any horses.'

The men seemed satisfied. All but Frank Hall. He said, 'Jason; you know what those men are. You've seen a hundred just as murderous in your time. Why won't you lend a hand?'

'Frank, I don't kill willingly. Even when I'm forced to it, I don't do it with pride or pleasure.'

'We don't kill for pleasure either, Jason.'

'But you make your own laws about it, Frank.'

Hall's jaw muscles rippled. He was a hard, not altogether temperate man; life had been a series of battles for him. He studied the massive man standing there watching him, then he said, 'Jason; if you'll provide fresh horses we'll fetch those three back alive. If you don't want to see justice done, we'll still get them on the animals we brought this far. An' we'll leave 'em hanging in the trees.'

Old Jason leaned on his shotgun. He looked

at all of them including Doc Heatly. 'The only way a country advances,' he said, 'is through the law, boys. Just because you don't hold with a law doesn't give you the right to break it. Change it if you will, but when you scorn it you're not one bit better'n the men you're after right now. You won't get any horses here unless you'll fetch back those nightriders to my yard alive, like Frank just said.'

Jess turned and darkly scowled as the possemen began to resentfully mutter. That youthful cowman from east of McAllister who'd never been in these wilds before, said, 'An' after we fetch 'em down here, Mister Weatherell, what then?'

'I'll go the rest of the way back to town with you, makin' plumb certain your prisoners arrive there alive, to be tried by a court o' law.'

Frank Hall glanced at the sun; they'd been standing around in Weatherell's yard nearly two hours. Before too much more time elapsed, dusk would be settling in. Evidently Jessica saw the way Frank was looking, and understood his thoughts for she said, 'They won't be much farther away in the morning, Mister Hall, than they are right now.'

Frank raised his eyebrows. 'Don't they know they're being trailed, Jess?'

'They know, but they're favouring their horses. If you think your animals are tuckered you should see theirs. It's a big, wild country,

56

Mister Hall; they'll try trading space for time with you; they were hunting rocky country when I turned back after watching them. They mean to hide their tracks, which will slow you down and at the same time allow them to rest a little.'

Pierson and Heatly exchanged a look. Doc left the girl's side to go over, lift his left stirrup-leather and begin loosening his cincha. Pete did the same. After a while Jess Palmer turned to also off-saddling. Finally, when Frank shrugged and walked over to his horse, all the others accepted his action as the final decision. Everyone turned to off-saddling.

Jason said something quiet to his girl and she walked away. Several of the men led their horses to the corrals and set them free, then ambled over to where a wooden pipe carried icy spring-water to a trough, bent down and slowly drank. Doc and Frank Hall came together over there to wash off the grit and silt. Frank said tonelessly, 'Be right careful, Doc. I know she's pretty as a picture, but Jason'll be havin' a dark eye on you.'

Heatly raised up and watched Frank sluice water a moment, then bent down and resumed washing. He didn't say a word.

Jess came over with several of the others. He was uncertain and said, 'I dunno. Seems to me we shouldn't be lyin' over here, Frank. Seems to me if we pushed straight on we'd be within pistol-range by tomorrow some time.'

Jason strolled on up and perched upon the edge of the trough, which was simply a large log hollowed out. He still held his scattergun, but now he was using it as a sort of support to lean upon. Up close, he was even more massive than he'd looked from the saddle. He rumbled at Jess, saying, 'Don't fret; Jess'll show you where they're heading come sunup, Jess. She'll lead you out an' around them so you boys can take 'em before noon.'

'I sure hope so,' said Jess. He finished washing and towelled off with a limp shirt-tail. 'Jason; you're being right unreasonable, you know. We've been friends for a long time so I'm sayin' this to you. Those fellers'll hang any way you look at it, down in McAllister or up here in the back-country.'

'Then let it be down in McAllister, Jess,' rumbled the big man, smiling benignly. 'An' it'll never be on your conscience—nor mine.' Jason stood up, looked over where a thin little spindrift of grey smoke was rising from a chimney at his house, and said, 'Jess's fixin' an early supper or a late dinner, boys, whichever you're a mind to call it. We'll eat and afterwards go fetch in the fresh animals.' He stood a moment thoughtfully considering his seven guests. 'I'm right sorry to hear about Fred,' he softly exclaimed. 'He was a right good man.'

Frank Hall turned, obviously going to use that statement for a basis to argue from again, but Jason doggedly wagged his head and Frank lost a little of his starch. He sighed, felt around for his makings and fell to manufacturing a smoke. Over the farthest peaks shadows formed and dropped straight down the slopes and into narrow, gloomy places. Frank lit up, stood quietly surveying the country roundabout, and never did push the argument.

When the men were cleaned up Jason took them around back to a small log hut and poured each of them a large cup full of cider. It wasn't laced cider, but pure apple cider made from Weatherell's own orchard and through his own big-wheeled cider press. While they were murmuring pleasurably that cowman from the eastern ranges beyond McAllister said, 'Somethin' I'd like to get straight, Mister Weatherell; when Mister Palmer's up here, an' your daughter's also around, an' you yell for Jess to fetch you a bucket o' water; which one gets there first?'

There was a little ripple of soft laughter among them. Jason smiled, his pitch-black eyes brightening amiably. 'Well, son,' he replied to the youthful cowman, 'my daughter was named for Jess Palmer. It's an old story an' goes back a good many years, but what it boils down to is that Jess Palmer came up here one late autumn when I was flat on my back with the internal colic, an' my wife was gone with the baby to her folks. It was all over for me until Mister Palmer showed up huntin' lost cattle.'

'I see,' said the cowman, looking down into his empty tin cup pointedly. 'An' he nursed you back to health.'

'Yes sir, son,' rumbled the massive, bearded man, reaching forth to take the rancher's cup and re-fill it. 'But more'n that; Jess Palmer sat there night after night by candlelight readin' to me from the Bible. I made a bargain with the Lord; if He'd pull me through, I'd serve Him right well.'

The others rolled their eyes around towards Jess; most of them looked accusingly at him. They clearly were thinking that if he'd read to Weatherell from some other book they wouldn't now be fouled up in their pursuit of the nightriders. Jess saw those looks and blushed a little. Then he said, by way of trite explanation, 'There wasn't anythin' else to read from.'

Jessica rang the triangle over at the main house summoning them to supper. They put down the tin cups and followed mighty Jason Weatherell back across the yard. Where those descending shadows now were, was farther down the mountainsides all around. Autumn dusks came early in the high country, and ordinarily cold came with them, but that high, hot wind must have still been blowing up there, for the evening was almost like late summer, except that it had a tangy scent to

60

it; a wild fragrance of congealing pine sap and drying grass and turning leaves.

That youthful cowman sidled up to old Jess Palmer and in a low hiss, said, 'Why'n hell didn't you just tell him stories?'

Jess hissed right back. 'Me, tell *him* stories? Randy; Jason Weatherell's done more things, fought more fights, run farther'n, jumped higher'n you an' me an' Frank Hall put together. Anyway; from the first time I met him running his trap lines up here forty year' back, he had that streak in him. I've seen him stand atop a hill with his arms out an' that beard o' his blowin' in the wind, talkin' to God like the redskins used to do.'

'Fat lot o' good it did them,' muttered the cowman, 'an' it's not goin' to help us either.'

Old Jess gave the younger man a roguish look. 'Just you wait, Randy,' he murmured as they came to the plank porch. 'Jessica'll lead us to 'em in the mornin' sure as you're a foot tall. Jason and his girl know these cussed mountains an' canyons better'n the Injuns ever did. You'll see.'

'Well I hope so,' growled the younger man. 'My wife'll raise Cain an' prop him up if I don't get home soon.'

The house was as massive and solid inside as it also was outside. Even the furnishings were three times as strong as was necessary. The fireplace was made of painstakingly hewn and squared blocks of Idaho grey granite, and

61

the firebox was large enough to roast half a steer in. It was definitely a house to match a man like Jason Weatherell; big and roomy and almost indestructible. The kitchen where they were fed was large, airy and had its own cooking fireplace as well as an ancient cast-iron black stove.

Everything was clean and Spartan. The men sat around an oaken table large enough to feed twice their numbers. Jessica laid out the food. To riders who'd been on the trail since the day before without food it was a banquet. Doc murmured admiration and Jessica coloured. She seemed more taken with Doc than with any of the others.

Jason asked a blessing before they ate, his shaggy head and great beard making him appear as some ancient patriarch right out of biblical times. Then he plunged in with a zest the others appreciated because they too were very hungry.

Doc didn't eat much, and after it was all over, he said he'd remain behind and help Jessica clean up while the others filed back outside for their final smoke of the day. It was the custom; rangeriders never smoked in a house unless their host did, and since Jason didn't use tobacco, they trooped out back where the sky was turning dark, to sigh and smoke and pleasurably pick their teeth.

There was a bluish aura over the farthest

peaks, and lower down the land lay dark-mantled and hushed. At this time of day it wasn't difficult to imagine why Jason preferred living his solitary life apart from the rest of the world. There and then, it seemed the only logical way for a man to live.

CHAPTER SEVEN

Doc and Jessica left the house by the front door and paced side by side through the bland evening, heading for the area down by the barn. She'd look up at him from time to time, and ask questions that no woman asked of a man unless her interest was more than simple curiosity. Why had he come with the others, she wanted to know; he didn't seem like a man who'd lean on a lynch-rope.

He drew her in where he paused to lean upon a corral pole watching their horses contentedly eating meadow hay, and told her his job was patching up the damage among men that the vengeance and justice of other men caused.

'Then you're not one of them that wants to lynch those nightriders,' she said, and leaned at his side looking far out where sky and earth merged.

His rebuttal came slow, each word carefully selected. 'I wouldn't say that, Jessica. I wouldn't say that I'd shed a tear or refuse to lend a hand on the hang-rope.' He turned and looked down into her greeny eyes. 'I reckon your father's right—up to a point—but he's attributing to Idaho a variety of justice which doesn't exist here, never has existed, and probably won't exist in your or my lifetime. Rule by law alone. Even in the fully civilised parts of our country rule by law is a fragile tenet, Jessica. Out here—lynch-law has its place in society.'

'It's wrong,' she murmured up to him. 'What right have these men to take three lives?'

'The same right, I'd say, that they have to defend themselves.'

'But they aren't being called on to defend themselves,' she argued, and he made a little gentle smile at her with his lips.

'But they will be called on to do it tomorrow, Jessica.' He reached over and very softly lay his hand atop hers without any pressure. 'You have a fine feeling for folks,' he said. 'Your father has too. But Jessica; this isn't a world where people are as they *should* be, not even back up here where you seldom see people. This is a world where men are as they allow themselves to become. Remember that, Jessica, if you ever leave your high country; it'll save you a lot of heart-ache.' He removed his hand and fell to gazing at the purple heavens.

She watched him for a while, evidently wondering more than ever about him. Finally she said, 'You mean—those men will fight tomorrow?'

He looked down and around. 'What choice have they? If they fight us back in here they might still get away. If they allow us to take them, they know as well as I know what'll happen to them down in McAllister where Fred Coffey was a popular man. They have one slim chance of getting clear, as opposed to three or four chances of dying—*if* they don't fight. Now tell me Jessica: Which would you do?'

She didn't answer. She turned away from him and put a long, brooding look over towards the house where her father had lighted some inside lanterns.

Doc also turned. He said candidly, 'I could use a drink.'

She roused herself and pointed over where the wooden pipe ran its steady trickle of cold spring water. He laughed quietly and let the topic drop; that hadn't been the kind of a drink he'd had in mind at all.

She said, 'Suppose I can put you men from McAllister into a position where those nightriders can't possibly fight you.'

'Good,' murmured Doc, his tone both dry and doubtful. 'That'll be fine. I'd as soon as we took them alive. Not because I feel any particular compassion, Jessica, but because if those three are as ornery as I think they might be, there's an excellent chance they might wound or kill some of the men who came this far with me.'

She straightened up off the corral looking thoughtful. She took his fingers in her hand and drew him along. They strolled through the fragrant gloom side by side, each very conscious of the other. Where she eventually halted was beyond the buildings where the nearest trace of forest stood darkly just beyond and higher, where there was a distinct paleness, a high cliff of grey stone stood up far back. That, she told him, was where the moon rose, beyond that grey stone face.

'It looks like a silent river flowing down the front, where that grey rock is,' she said, releasing his fingers. 'I wanted you to see it.'

He looked up there, then down at her profile. There wasn't a flaw that he could discern. Where her throat terminated the lift of her breasts began, and lower, her stomach was as flat as a man's stomach. He resumed the waiting and watching. But it wasn't the rising moon that suddenly galvanised him into action, it was another kind of reflected light; the eerie, black shine of starlight off gun metal. He saw it up there through the forest and lunged against her bearing her violently to the ground. She struggled, turning huge eyes upwards as he clamped a hand across her lips.

'Quiet,' he whispered, bending low over

her. 'Be quiet. Now turn your head very slowly and look up past the first rank of those northward trees.' He withdrew his hand and settled still lower upon the ground. She rolled her head as he'd said, straining to see, but evidently the man out there had moved for even when Doc looked, he couldn't find that naked gun again.

She turned her head towards him, more puzzled than alarmed. 'Are you sure?' she whispered, her heavy mouth brushing the side of his face near the ear. 'Did you see a gun?'

He nodded. 'I know a gun when I see one. Now listen to me; we're exposed out here. He dassn't move. He's probably gone on around to the west and south, down through the trees as far as he can towards the house. We don't dare move until we're sure he's ahead of us.'

She suddenly jerked as though to arise. He flung an arm across her chest holding her down. She said, 'We've got to warn the others.'

'How,' he said irritably, 'by jumping up and getting shot? Lie still until I tell you to move.'

Her breathing was hard and rapid. He could feel it beneath his restraining arm, so he moved clear of her, very carefully raised his head, took a long look all around, then sank down again.

'I think we're safe,' he whispered, his face less than six inches from hers. 'Give him another minute, then we'll make a try for it.'

'Who was he, George?'

'I don't know. I never got a look at him. Only his gun as he was moving. What's more important for us, he didn't get a look at us either.'

'Are you armed?' she whispered.

He raised his head and looked at her. They were very close. He didn't answer right away. Instead, he slowly, very tenderly lowered his face and brushed those heavy, dark lips with his mouth, and breathed a rough statement. 'What a hell of a way to fall in love, Jessica . . . No; I'm not armed. I'm a doctor, not a gunfighter or a rangerider.'

He rolled away once and looked up. She didn't move; just her misty green eyes followed him, their expression disturbed, hungry, full of strange lights and shadows. He turned and beckoned. She moved a little, got up and crept over to him. Then she waited, but he did not turn to look at her again; he got both legs under him saying, 'Get set, Jessica; we can make the barn if we're lucky and if he's far enough southward not to see us start out. Don't run straight. Cut back and forth as you go. Are you ready?'

'Yes.'

He got up into a low crouch, one knee stiffened to complete the jump to his feet, the other knee still upon the ground. Somewhere, a man was stalking Jason Weatherell's house with his gun drawn and ready. He'd probably hear Doc and the girl even if he did not at once catch sight of them, but there was nothing else for it.

Doc said: 'Now!' and sprang up, turned, let Jessica rush past, then ran along in her wake. For a hundred feet the ground was grassy and muffled their footfalls, but beyond that where the earth had been tramped hard by men and animals, they made a recognizable sound. But the barn was close, too, and it also was between them and about where Doc Heatly thought that armed stranger had to be.

He was right, but only partly so. They lacked twenty feet of reaching the barn when the first smashing explosion and lancing red flash of gun-flame rang out. Lead struck the log barn wall a foot to their left and on ahead of them. Doc reacted by grabbing Jessica and violently jerking her to the far right.

The next bullet sang straight down through the barn and hit a jumble of harness hanging there; the chain traces rattled.

From up at the house a man's sudden, sharp outcry rang through the gloom.

Doc held tightly when he passed inside the barn, almost dragging Jessica with him. He lunged backwards too, so they'd be protected by the jutting corner of that massive front wall. It was a good precaution because the third shot fired in their direction struck solidly making a meaty, ripping sound.

Jessica went up against Doc and lay there.

He put both arms around her pressing her still tighter to him, moving back with her until there wasn't much chance of either of them being struck.

At the house the unmistakable bull-bass roar of Jessica's father rang out, calling for his daughter and Doc. Frank Hall also cried out, his voice raspish and rough-sounding.

No more shots came right away.

Doc pushed Jessica aside and faced her. 'Is there a gun in here?' he asked.

She nodded. 'On those saddles your friends dumped in here when they turned their horses out.'

'Get one,' he snapped, then changed that order. 'Get two. I'll see where he is.'

Jessica slipped away and was at once lost in the darkness of the big old log barn. Doc inched forward and looked out back where the trees came within a hundred yards of the building. There was nothing moving out there, nothing to be seen at all. He stepped back when Jessica came up with their carbines and pushed one into his hand.

He looked closely at her. 'Now what do you think of them?' he demanded. 'They've come back for fresh horses.'

'They?' she murmured. 'But I left them five miles out looking for rockslides to lose their tracks in.'

'Who else?' he hissed. 'Is there anyone else who'd try drygulching like this?'

She didn't answer, but she stepped around him and sank to one knee while she peered over into the trees. At the house her father bellowed again and this time Doc answered, to let him know where Jessica was and that they were safe. After that it got deathly silent all around.

Up at the main-house the men from McAllister had surmised what was occurring, and Jason had doused those lanterns he'd lighted. As time ran silently on Doc got uneasy. The only horses around that he knew of were the ones he and his friends had corralled out back. Otherwise, there were several stalled animals in the barn. Clearly, those killers out there weren't after the tucked-up beasts of the possemen, which meant they'd concentrate on the animals in the barn—providing they knew there were horses in there.

Doc knelt close and touched Jessica's shoulder. 'When they were here earlier,' he asked, 'did they happen to enter this barn?'

She turned and nodded, waiting for him to say more, but he didn't. He merely sighed, waggled his head and resumed his vigil of the yonder night.

The moon came. It glided noiselessly up from below that grey-granite cliff-face she'd shown him out there to the north. It was only half full but that was enough because of the clear, pure high-country air. Light fell down in a ghostly way to limn the buildings, the yonder gloomy forest, and across the yard where six men and Jason Weatherell crouched, waiting.

She turned, saying, 'We call it a nightrider's moon, George.'

He nodded; it was an apt term. Then he thought of something else and said, 'How'd you know my name?'

'Uncle Jess told me,' she murmured, looking swiftly away from him back out towards the dark trees. 'I asked him. Is it all right?'

He smiled at her. 'My name, or that you asked him? Sure it's all right.'

She reached for his hand and gave it a hard squeeze, then resumed her sentinel duty of watching. He also considered the trees, wondering whether all three of them were over there, or whether all this silence meant the other two were manoeuvring around to perhaps get a clean shot from over across the yard. He started to stand up; to walk away from the back of the barn where Jessica would keep watch, when a gun roared and lead struck the wall outside very close to where Jessica was kneeling. She jumped clear of that place and moved instantly around where some saddlery lay in a heap.

'We've got to keep them out of here,' she said. 'George; if they get these horses we'll never even see them again. All our other stock's a long way off I deliberately pushed them away when we knew strangers were coming.'

'You,' he told her, pointing a finger, 'stay away from that rear doorway. I'm going up front. Your paw and the others'll understand what those nightriders are after. They'll try to reach us down here.'

'The other two,' she whispered insistently. 'There's only one out back in the trees; where are those other two?'

'I hope not around front,' he murmured, and slipped away from her heading up towards the front doorway.

The men at the main-house hadn't fired a single shot yet. Obviously, they had discerned no targets to fire at. Doc could see the main-house and all the outbuildings from his crouched position by the front barn entrance. There wasn't a sign of life anywhere. It was eerie, being unable to see anyone, and yet knowing perfectly well that there were nearly a full dozen armed men out there in the night waiting to kill one another.

CHAPTER EIGHT

The speculation about the other two night-riders was resolved for Doc and Jessica when up near the main-house an unseen drygulcher opened up suddenly and savagely, peppering the house, breaking windows, firing off round after round.

Doc had no way of knowing whether or not that man had actual targets to blaze away at, but because of the wildly furious style of the nightrider's shooting, he doubted it.

Doc got down very gingerly and looked around the corner of the barn's front doorway. It had been his desire to locate the man up near the house by muzzleblast. But from within the house came a volley of return-fire which either completely silenced the attacker up there, or drove him away, but in either event Doc didn't see where he'd been firing from.

But the third man almost succeeded where his friends had not come off so well. He was directly across from the barn crouching beside a dark log shed of some kind, completely covered by darkness when he fired straight through the barn from front to back, shifted his aim slightly and did the same thing a second and third time. His strategy was clear enough; he knew at least two defenders were inside that old barn. He logically reasoned those two would be crouching at either the front or rear entrance, keeping watch. So he'd fired three separate shots, one to the right, one to the left, and one centre.

He hadn't hit anyone, but if Doc and Jessica weren't extremely careful, if he kept it up, he eventually would hit someone.

Still; the odds were in favour of the defenders. Even Doc and old Jason's daughter in the barn had shelter, guns and ammunition. At the main-house they also had numerical superiority as well as plenty of bullets and guns. Doc was waiting for that man over across the yard to fire again, so he could aim at his gun-flame; while he waited he assessed their chances all around and decided that if the men from McAllister hadn't been there, the nightriders would've added two more murders to their score of killings, but coming back as they had to force Jason to give them fresh horses, they probably hadn't expected so many guns to be aligned against them.

But regardless of all other considerations, unless they kept the defenders pinned down, eventually seven men were going to get away from the Weatherell ranch and go after the nightriders. Only now, when they took up the fresh trail, they'd have an added incentive to push on.

There was no more firing. Doc left off speculating and returned his full attention to the here-and-now. Jessica came noiselessly up to him near the front of the barn. She said it was too quiet out there. He told her to go back and keep watch. He also risked a slow look out and around. There wasn't any movement anywhere, not even up at the main-house where he was confident his acquaintances were peering out into the night just as hard

75

as he also was.

Time ran on, the hush became oppressive, Doc went back to stand by Jessica for a while, saying nothing but gauging the yonder night, while elsewhere that increasing and lengthening silence built up all around the ranchyard until Doc said, 'I don't understand . . . Unless they've pulled out I can't imagine what they're up to.'

Jess shook her head. 'There were too many of us. They had to give it up.' She grounded her carbine and lifted her eyes to him. 'They didn't get in here, George, did they?'

He smiled at her. 'Sure didn't, Jess. Didn't even come close.'

Evidently up at the house the others came to that same conclusion because Jess Palmer piped up, calling shrilly to the barn. 'Doc? Jessica? Anybody else down there?'

'No one else,' sang out Doc. 'Can you see anything up there?'

'All quiet,' answered Palmer, and ceased speaking for a while.

Frank Hall called down to the barn next. 'Doc; listen to me. This is Frank. We're comin' down to you, so hold your fire. All of us are comin' down to the barn. Don't shoot, Doc. You hear me?'

'We hear you, Frank,' answered Heatly, and turned to stroll back across towards the front barn entrance. 'Be careful; just because they aren't firing doesn't mean they aren't

76

waiting for something like this.'

It was an unnecessary warning from Doc to the men at the house, but he called it to them anyway, then he took position, waiting and watching. The silence went on, deeper and more enduring with each passing moment. Doc didn't see the men up there leave the house, but that did not particularly surprise him; he'd competently sized-up Jason. If there was a canny way to get from the house to the barn, old Jason would show them, and that's precisely how it worked out.

Frank Hall and Jason appeared around the southeast corner of the barn not fifty feet away. Frank said: 'Doc? That you at the doorway?'

Heatly replied that it was him. He'd been surprised at those men showing up like that, so suddenly and without any advance notice. 'Come ahead,' he said.

They came in a swift rush, Jason lunging ahead out front, Frank behind him. Jess and Pete next, and the cowman from east of McAllister, the man old Jess called Randy, bringing up the rear. Doc didn't say anything until they were all inside, Jason and his daughter coming together down near the rear doorway, then he caught Frank's arm and gave it as his opinion that the three renegades had departed some time earlier.

Frank bitterly inclined his head. 'They got no fresh mounts,' he said. 'But I reckon this was still their go-round.'

Doc raised his eyebrows. Jess and Pete Pierson came stalking up looking as bitter in the face as Frank also looked.

'We're all that's left,' said old Jess Palmer. 'Take a good look, Doc. You'n me an' Randy, Frank, Pete—that's all, Doc.'

'Only five of us?' said Doc. 'There were a...'

'Yeah, we know,' Frank nodded. 'They're lying up there on Jason's front porch, dead. They figured to try gettin' down here to help you'n Jessica. That's when all that wild shootin' broke out up there a while back. One of the nightriders was positioned to watch the house. He got 'em before they even got off the porch, damn his lights!'

Doc stood quietly for a moment, then turned and started out of the barn. Pierson would have stopped him but Jess said, 'Let him go; they aren't out there any more. Besides, Doc's quite a feller for tryin' to coax life back into folks.'

Jason and his daughter came up where the others were glumly standing. For a while no one had much to say. Jason eventually rallied and suggested they all go up to the house. No one dissented; no one actually thought much about it one way or another. Jason led off with Jessica at his side still carrying that carbine she'd been using at the barn. When they got to the porch Doc was standing there

78

making a smoke, his face shadowed by the tipped-down brim of his hat. Behind him were two very dead townsmen, the last of that little contingent of clerks and merchants who'd joined the cattlemen back at McAllister.

Doc lit up, exhaled, looked at them all and shook his head. 'Whoever he was, out there, he was a dead shot.'

Frank nodded. He'd evidently also examined the corpses. Jason said in his deep-down drum-roll voice, 'I'll see to their burials in the morning. Best to let them lie where they are for now. Come into the house.'

Doc was the last one to enter. He propped that Winchester he'd gotten back at the barn, in a corner, and hung his droopy dark hat over the barrel. Randy and Pete Pierson sank down upon chairs looking morose. Frank watched Jason and his girl leave the room, then he said, 'Well; the odds're sure gettin' whittled down, boys. Any of you want to call it quits?'

No one replied to the question, but Pierson said, 'You didn't give Weatherell your word, Frank. I say let's get the fresh animals and be ready to move out the second it's light enough to see by. Let's find 'em an' get this done and over with.'

The others nodded approval of everything Pete had said. Doc didn't nod, but he didn't have anything contrary to say either.

Hall went to a window and gazed out into the blackness. The moon was somewhere

79

down behind the house softly lighting the southward mountains and prairies. Frank's tough lined old weathered countenance was set in a harsh, merciless fashion. 'I didn't give him my word,' he said without facing the others. 'But if we take his horses we're honour-bound to bring those nightriders back alive.'

Pierson had the bleak answer for that, too. He said, 'Then let's use our own animals. They'll be fairly well rested and filled out by sunup. But Frank; I'm against even taking those murderers alive, let alone fetching them all the way back down to McAllister to be tried.'

Jason and his daughter returned to the parlour. One with a lighted coal-oil lantern, the other carrying a big graniteware coffee pot and a stack of tin mugs. Neither of them said a word until they were pouring the cups full and handing them around. Then Jason ran a slow, black gaze around at the bitter-faced possemen and spoke quietly.

'I'll go with you, come sunup. Jess'll come too. I don't want to leave her behind after what they tried here tonight. That's a treacherous trio.'

The possemen were silent for a while, eyeing Jason and sipping hot coffee, until Pete Pierson said, 'Mister Weatherell; maybe you'd better not come along. You nor your girl.' He didn't explain why; he didn't have to, everyone in the room understood well enough.

Jason cocked an eye at the light; it was smoking. He stood up to his full height dwarfing everyone else in the room to adjust the lamp-wick. 'I understand,' he murmured. 'But I expect Jess an' I'll ride along with you anyway.'

No one argued. In fact no one spoke again for a long while. The reaction set in hard; men relaxed nursing their cups of java, looking everywhere but at one another, remembering those two dead men out there. Also remembering Fred Coffey. The night ran on like that, dark and brooding and hushed.

Doc made a smoke to give his hands something to do, popped it between his lips but never lighted it. Jessica was watching him from a shadowy corner over near the door leading to the pantry and kitchen, her face composed and gentle-looking.

Frank took a gold watch from his pocket, flipped the case open, studied the spidery hands a moment then closed the case and put the timepiece away. 'Three o'clock,' he said. 'Jason; what time does decent light show up around here?'

'Four-thirty this late in the year, Frank. No later'n five. It wouldn't hurt if we went down to the barn and grained the horses.'

Frank nodded and stepped away from the window. The others sluggishly prodded themselves up to their feet. They walked out of the house. Doc lingered and across the room

Jessica stood still.

She said, 'I know what you're thinking. You believe my father is going along to prevent a lynching.'

'Isn't he?' asked Doc, softly smiling across the big room at her.

'He'll want to prevent that if he can, yes. But I know him better than anyone else does. He's fought some of his most savage battles right here in this yard, in the early years when my mother was alive. He never permitted anyone to attack his ranch without paying dearly for it.'

Doc removed the un-lighted cigarette and went over to get his hat. He tossed the cigarette into the fireplace and settled the hat atop his head. Then he turned towards the door.

'Come along,' he murmured, but she shook her head at him.

'I'll make up a sack of food, then I'll be along.' She waited until he had a hand upon the latch, then quietly said, 'George . . . ?' He turned. 'What you said out there—before we got to the barn . . .'

'I meant it, Jess. I meant every word of it. But it's only fair to tell you you could do a lot better than me. I'm thirty-five years old. Probably better than ten years older than you are. On top of that, I drink. And if that isn't enough to scare you off . . .' He paused, considered her from a distance of

82

nearly thirty feet in golden lamp-light, then said, 'Regardless of all that, though, Jess; I'd cherish you.' Then he opened the door, stepped through and gently closed it after him.

There was a hint of pre-dawn chill to the night air outside. The moon was well along on its down-grade side but the stars up there were even brighter than before. Down at the barn a lantern flickered; tall, elongated man-shadows moved back and forth. A long way off in the direction of that grey-stone bluff Jessica had shown him, a wolf gave tongue to the dying night, and closer, a fox made its sharp little repetitive bark.

Doc glanced at the pair of dead men. He was impersonal towards them. He'd known both men in life, but once life departed they became something professionally unchallenging and not to be identified with friends any longer. He stepped around them and started down across the yard towards the barn. He stopped though, looked back, then retraced his steps to the porch and silently lugged those corpses around the side of the house where a small shed stood, and deposited them both in there.

Finally, he trudged down to the barn. It had crossed his mind that if Jason and Jessica went with the riders from McAllister, after the bushwhackers, only the Lord knew when—or even *if*—they'd all return, and those two bodies shouldn't be left out there in the open like that.

Frank Hall emerged from the barn just as Doc walked on up. Frank put a wry look over and said quietly, 'Don't forget what I told you at the trough, Doc. Trifle with her an' old Jason'll split your breastbone clear through.'

'He doesn't believe in killing, Frank.'

Hall's lips quirked in a cold little grin. 'Oh yes he does, Doc. Don't let all that talk kid you. Jason'll kill as quick as the next man. Only he's got to feel thoroughly justified. I'd say there's nothin' on this earth that'd make the old devil feel more justified than if he figures someone was triflin' with his girl.'

Doc and Frank stood there gazing straight at one another. Heatly eventually said, 'I'm not trifling, Frank.'

Hall's answer was prompt. 'In that case let me be the first to congratulate you.' His smile perked up, turned warm and at the same time teasing. 'Although I got to admit I'll be doggoned if I didn't always figure she'd pick some brawny hell-for-leather buckaroo.'

'Thanks,' replied Doc, smiling at the bronzed, lean old horseman.

Jess came out to them. He ran a slow look up along the peaks and rims. 'Wish to hell it'd get light,' he mumbled.

Frank nodded. 'Yeah. 'Hope findin' out we were all here tonight didn't scare those boys bad enough to make 'em ride all night gettin' away.'

Doc said, 'Frank; Jess; what do you think our chances are?'

Frank's answer was first. 'No question about that, Doc; we'll get 'em. I promise you we'll get 'em. The question is—when.'

Jess nodded and kept on studying the skyline. He didn't say anything right away, but eventually he did. 'We'll get 'em, Doc. An' may the Lord have mercy on their souls when we do. Let's get mounted; it's dang near light enough.'

CHAPTER NINE

They left the Weatherell place seven strong, counting Jessica and old Jason. The Weatherell horses they rode carried an arrowhead branded on each left shoulder. They were fine, stout beasts, the kind of mounts any horseman, even Frank Hall, could take pride in forking.

Jess and her father rode out front. Once, when Doc said something about the danger to Jessica, Jason put a level, black look upon him and said she'd be all right up there; that they'd cover a lot of ground before they'd even be close to the nightriders.

That was proven quite correct. They were far back through some desolate, wild and gloomy canyons before the sun finally arose, bringing on a good warmth again, but before it had climbed much higher they were underneath the northerly rims crossing a huge plateau where elk-grass and alders proved that regardless of appearances, there was shallow water beneath them. Neither Frank nor Jess were very familiar with the country on westward. Each admitted they'd been up in there a time or two, but said it had been a good many years back on hunting trips. No cattle, it seemed, ever drifted this far into the wilds.

'Too many varmints,' explained Jess to Doc and Pete Pierson who were riding along on each side of him.

'There's more cussed bears and big cats up in here than there were when the redskins owned it all.'

Jason and Jessica split up, on ahead, quartering back and forth where rock showed through the thin soil as bleached and grey as old bones. They'd lost the trail. Doc watched out there where they came together again, marvelling at the closeness they shared, and also at the way Jessica handled her horse and herself on this grim manhunt.

She had a Colt Lightning sixshooter belted to her small waist. She also had a thirty-thirty in the scabbard under her right fender, butt forward and purposefully slung so that it rode within inches of her free right hand. She rode in the traditional fashion of the West; always with the reins in the left hand.

Jason loped out ahead to the north. Jessica went off, also at a lope, to the south. They bypassed the place where the nightriders had effectively hidden their tracks, and eventually picked up the sign again a mile away. There, they waited, resting their animals, until the other riders got close, then whirled and trotted off again without a word.

'Like a pair of Indians,' said Randy to old Jess Palmer. 'That girl sure can sit a saddle.'

'She ought to be able to,' muttered Jess, and added nothing to that comment as he raised an arm pointing to some jagged, jutting rimrocks dead ahead a couple of miles. 'If I was one of those nightriders that's where I'd be right now —waitin' an' watchin'.'

Jason dropped from sight far out. Jessica did the same. That was how the possemen knew the plateau they had been crossing with the sun upon their ribs, ended down in another of those weedy canyons.

But at least this particular canyon wasn't so deep nor narrow it taxed their horses, and when they were upon its northerly rim Jason and his daughter were waiting, standing by their horses. Frank and Doc rode up first. Jason pointed to the ground. A soiled, red-stained bandage lay where fresh horsetracks marked the route of the outlaws.

'One of 'em didn't walk off unmarked last night,' Jason said, then toed in and sprang up across his saddle as he looked up towards the yonder jutting rimrocks. 'But it wasn't a bad wound.'

'How d'you know that?' Randy asked, squinting down at the discarded bandage. 'There's plenty of blood on those rags.'

Doc answered him. 'That's frothy blood, Randy, not thick and dark red. It's a superficial injury.'

Jason turned and gazed a moment at Doc, then faced ahead without a word and rode on. Jessica threw him an approving smile before she also led out.

For ten or fifteen minutes Jason let his horse pick its own gait while he slouched in the saddle stroking his beard and thoughtfully studying those overhead peaks. When he'd made up his mind about whatever point he'd been puzzling over, he lifted the reins and turned southward, bringing the entire cavalcade parallel with those scowling dark cliffs. He'd abandoned the nightrider's trail completely and Randy said something tart about this, but Frank Hall threw the younger man an annoyed look and nothing more was said.

Doc privately thought Jason was embarking upon some kind of a gamble; he knew these mountains. Evidently he'd come to a conclusion respecting the progress or the route of the men they were after, and was now heading southward for some definite interception. But he neither asked Jason, nor said anything about this to the others, as they went along in the shadowy lee of that enormous stone bluff to a stand of poplar trees, and there watered their livestock at a clear-water, ice-cold spring.

Here, Jessica took down her chuck bag and handed food around. Here too, Jason said it would be all right to kill a few minutes, so everyone gratefully got down, sat in poplar-shade, ate and drowsed and filled up on good water.

The trail from this place continued southward to where that high cliff dwindled down into a serrated series of low hills, some with trees dotting them, some as bald as a billiard table, but with wild grasses and flowers flourishing in the late, warm autumn haze.

Jason said something to his girl. Jessica loped ahead, swerved over behind a jutting promontory, and disappeared. When the others came up to this spot they found a broad old trail leading straight through the thick shouldered, low hills, into a broad, wild valley beyond. As they emerged from that secret pass, Jason reined up, sat perfectly still for a long time looking all around, then, as Jessica loped back he said, 'Well; it was a hard decision. If they'd known this country—which I was gambling they didn't—they'd have had enough moonlight last night to get down this far from behind those rimrocks back there, where their tracks went.' He looked at his daughter. She mutely shook her head in reply to his unasked question, and old Jason smiled with what Doc thought was grand relief.

'They're north of us, boys. We're below the route they're coming down-country.' Jason gestured around with one mighty arm. 'It's mostly open country out there. We can crawl through the grass an' waylay them, or we can go another mile southward where the valley ends and pinches down, get into the rocks and stop them down there. Which'll it be?'

'Go south and waylay 'em in the rocks,' said Frank Hall, without any hesitation. 'That's the only pass down out of here, as I recollect.'

'Dead right,' agreed Jason, and nodded for Jessica to lead the way. 'Stay close to this sidehill,' he cautioned her. 'They could still see us moving if we got out where the sunlight shown.'

To reach that rocky place Jason and Frank had spoken of they had to cross several shale fields where each hoof-fall rattled loudly in the deep hush of this uplands place, but the noise didn't seem to bother Jason, so the others had nothing to say about it.

Jessica led them, always staying in the gloom of the western slope. She brought them down to where that slope, which was on their right, dwindled right down into a jumbled bed of volcanic boulders, some as large and thick as a horse, but generally smaller and rounder and with their lower parts solidly buried in several feet of grassy sod. Here, they started a big six-point buck out of his bed. He sprang away with a loud thump and an equally as loud snort. He ran down where the dusty trail passed through the boulderfield and within moments was lost to sight. But his route had shown the men exactly where the trail passed through the rocks, which was important.

Jessica dismounted, led her horse over behind several huge rocks, and returned moments later without the animal, but with her carbine. She and Jason stood briefly in conversation, then she worked her way up through the men and halted where Doc Heatly was standing beside his horse gazing back up that golden-lighted broad expanse of tall, cured grass.

'They'll have to come this way,' she informed him. 'Whether they find the trail right away or not will determine whether we see them within the next half hour, or not, but there's no other trail down out of here.'

Doc pointed off to the southwest where some sagebrush low hills looked both low and amenable to travel. 'What's on the far side of those hills?' he asked.

'A sandstone cliff,' she said, and smiled up at him. 'If they go that way, they'll still have to turn east and come over here; there's just no other way out. My father and I have trapped wild horses up here. We never failed when the horses ran for this meadow.' She reached for his reins. 'We'd better hide your horse. Every other animal is out of sight.'

Doc trailed along behind her over into the westerly boulders and secured his animal to a scraggly juniper tree where cool shade made him pause. All around, upon the slopes and benches, frost had touched wild grapes and buckbrush, turning the leaves yellow and scarlet and vivid red. The whole wild high country was a blaze of riotous colour. He said, 'Jessica; it would be hard for a person born and reared in this, to leave it.'

She nodded, not looking at him, but also gazing out where all that profligate natural beauty was. Then she said something that brought his eyes lower down, to her profile. She said, 'A person must always follow their star, George. I remember my mother saying that to me a long time ago, when I was very young. At the time I didn't understand. But I sure understand now.' She raised her eyes to his. 'But I could come back, couldn't I, George?'

'Every autumn,' he said. 'It would be like committing a crime not to. Both of us?'

'Both of us,' she murmured, and swiftly turned to walk out where her father and the others were talking in a little tight group, every man with his naked carbine in hand. Doc followed, also lugging a Winchester.

Jason had just finished explaining about this

place. 'It's their only way,' he was saying. 'So, whether they like it or not, as long as they keep travelling southward, they'll come to us.' He lifted his jet black gaze and scanned the empty northward plain. 'What I'm wonderin' is whether, when they get up close, they'll have the good sense to quit.'

Jess said, 'Jason; that's our end of it. You've just done your work. From here on the rest of us'll take over.'

Jason dropped his gaze to old Jess's hard-scarred fist where it was tight-closed around the carbine. 'No,' he said. 'They hit my ranch last night, Jess. They could've shot down my girl. I've made a lifelong practice of settling with men who attacked me or mine.'

Jess cleared his throat and spat, but didn't say anything. He didn't look the least bit relenting though. Frank Hall and Randy were carefully checking weapons a few feet distant. When Frank finished he looked straight at old Jason and said, 'I agreed to fetch 'em back alive, Jason, which you asked. But let's get somethin' straight right now so we'll have no arguments later. They get one chance to throw away their guns. I'll hail 'em—but they only get that one chance. If one of 'em goes for a gun . . .' Frank didn't finish; he didn't have to. His bronzed, lean face was set in a tough, uncompromising manner. He and Jason looked squarely at one another for a long interval.

93

'Let me talk to them,' Jason said. 'My voice'll carry farther, Frank.'

Hall looked around Doc nodded. So did Jess and Pete Pierson. Randy neither nodded nor dissented; it didn't seem to matter much to him who called on the nightriders to give up. His expression said very clearly that he didn't expect them to comply no matter who called to them nor what he said.

'All right,' Frank assented. 'But keep down, Jason. These aren't bronco bucks out to steal a few ponies an' maybe bushwhack a wood-cutter or two.'

Jason smiled indulgently at Frank. Without saying it, he was obviously thinking that he'd been through more bad spots like this one than Frank had; he knew how to handle himself.

Jessica went over where Doc was leaning upon a huge rock. 'Is this where we hide?' she asked.

'I reckon so,' Doc replied. 'But if you so much as raise your head I'll take a switch to you.'

She softly laughed up at him.

CHAPTER TEN

Time passed, the heat increased slightly in among those boulders and Randy got fidgety and had trouble sitting still. Every

94

few minutes he'd arise, step out for a look around, then step back with a muttered curse and wag his head. No one said anything to him; the others were older men, mostly seasoned, experienced, hardened to the long waits and violent subsequent actions in life. They smoked and visited a little, and occasionally eyed the sun or craned around to perhaps sight a dust-banner which would indicate horsemen were coming.

Doc and Jessica gave the impression, sitting close over there among their private rockfield, that they couldn't have been less concerned whether the nightriders ever came at all, or not.

But they were coming. The last time Randy poked his head out to mutteringly look around, he became quite still and abruptly very silent. Frank called quietly over to him asking if he saw anything. Randy nodded, watched a little longer, then glided back out of sight over where the older man sat in pleasant grey shade.

'Three horsemen coming over the middle rise out there,' he reported. 'Anglin' what looks to me to be south-easterly.'

The others started to move but Jason got up first and gestured for his companions to stay down. He stepped through some rocks west of the trail, leaned for a long time upon a particular piece of pocked lava-stone, then came back.

'It's them all right, and they're heading over towards the sagebrush hills on down the meadow. But there's a big sandstone cliff down the far side of it. They'll have to see that when they get atop the ridge. Then they'll have to drift right down towards us from the west.' He looked around seemingly making an appraisal of their position. He pointed towards the rocks on the east side of the trail. 'Maybe it'd be better was we all to get over there. At least when the showdown comes, we'll be in there and they won't be *able* to get hidden among those same rocks.'

The men agreed, arose, dusted off, and started across the trail. As each man hesitated before stepping out into the clearing, he looked northward where three moving silhouettes showed far out, bearing slightly away from them. Frank Hall called to Doc and Jessica.

In their fresh positions the men could watch those nightriders all the way across the meadow and up along the far sagebrush slopes, but beyond appearing as mounted individuals they were as yet too far for anything particular to be noticeable about them as men. This made a perfectly impersonal assessment by the hiding waylayers possible, for as yet their enemies were only moving objects. It would be some little time yet before those horsemen became anything else.

Jess Palmer told Jason Weatherell he

thought they'd have a battle on their hands if they challenged the nightriders first, before laying into them. Jason reared up, bristling.

'Jess; do you mean to lie here and tell me after all these years I've mis-judged you: That you'd shoot those men down in cold . . . ?'

'Consarn it no,' interrupted Jess, looking indignant. 'All I'm sayin' is, what've they got to lose? O' course they won't surrender.'

Frank called everyone's attention to the fact that those three men had now reached the ridge atop their sagebrush hill. 'They've stopped up there,' said Frank. 'Watch them now.'

Even Doc and Jessica rose up to peer ahead where brilliant sunlight showed those three as still and motionless as statues. Gradually, the man in the lead turned to ride slowly along the ridge, heading around towards the east. Jessica eased down gently and looked at Doc. He looked straight back. Neither of them smiled nor spoke. Their enemies were coming straight towards them now, but even that wasn't what caused their gravity. Unless something unusual and unexpected happened very soon, those nightriders were going to ride straight into the same kind of ambush they'd proven themselves so adept at establishing. After that . . .

'George? Will they surrender?'

Doc shook his head. 'I'm willing to bet a thousand dollars they won't.'

'Well then . . .' she murmured, and dropped her eyes away from him as she slowly turned her head and gazed out where the riders were coming straight along atop the ridge.

'Don't waste your pity,' he told her. 'They don't deserve it.'

'They deserve a chance, though.'

'Sure, and they'll get their chance. But I doubt if they'll take it.'

Jason twisted to look around. He didn't say so, but evidently he was interested in making certain his companions were low enough so they couldn't be seen. He needn't have worried; these were not altogether greenhorns.

The sun's brightness began to fade a little, to become vaguely obscure. No one had noticed it but a definite cloudy cast had come across the heavens, transparent and fleecy, but unmistakably the precursor to some change in the weather. And it became very still. The humidity raised. It got quite warm along with being so still and leaden and diaphanously fog-like high up in the heavens.

Frank and Jess cocked seasoned eyes. As cowmen their thoughts were never actually very far removed from consideration of the weather. Now, they scanned that murky sky and turned to make certain its peculiar milkiness stretched all the way across.

'Autumn's about over,' murmured Jess. 'Frank; it could hit tonight. What d'you figure?'

'The same,' agreed Hall. 'What I'm wonderin' is whether there's a big cold-front behind this, or whether there just might be another desert wind. If it's a hot wind we're all right.'

'And,' rumbled Jason, also studying the changing sky, 'If it's a cold-front boys, we'll want to be back down at my place before morning.'

This peculiar, subtle change in the weather seemed to go un-noticed by the outlaws walking their horses eastward along the ridge. They were much more interested in how to get off their headland and down to the southward plains beyond.

They were only about a mile off now, and still coming. Randy shielded his eyes the better to individually study them. None of the others bothered; the nightriders would get close enough directly. Pete Pierson crept through tall rocks and settled sweatily beside Doc. 'That bottle you had,' he began, and Doc began sadly wagging his head back and forth at Pierson. 'You mean,' asked Pete forlornly, 'We finished it?'

'We did, Pete. There's a canteen of water hanging on my saddle you're welcome to it if . . .'

'I don't need a bath,' growled Pierson, and went scuttling back over where he'd come from.

The horsemen were close enough now to

make out that one of them had a bandage around his lower left arm, above the wrist and below the elbow. He rode along as though the wound were painful, now and then lifting the arm and shoving it into the front of his un-buttoned shirt. Jess murmured something about that and Frank nodded. Jason watched that man intently for a long while, until the trio was almost within gun range, but he said nothing to the others about whatever interested him.

Doc removed his hat, got down between two dark spires and put one eye to the narrow cleft between them to also watch. Once, he slowly turned and looked around to see what Jessica was doing. She was crouched in behind a smooth old piece of sandstone half as high as she'd have been had she been standing.

They were close enough, finally, and old Jason sucked down a deep breath and hailed them, his drum-roll bass booming back and forth among the rocks and fluting up the yonder hillside. The second he spoke, those three men up there froze; hauled back suddenly on their reins, and froze.

'Boys; you're covered by seven guns. You're well within range an' you're exposed. It'll be up to you an' the Lord. Sit still and keep your hands in plain sight an' you'll come through. Start anything an' you'll be dead before you hit the ground. This is Jason Weatherell. We met down at my ranch yesterday—and last night when you tried to raid me. The men with me are from McAllister; the same ones that've been trailing you since you shot Sheriff Coffey.'

Jason stopped speaking. Frank's carbine barrel made a rough sound as he abrasively slid it along the top of his rock, hunched close around the gun. Jason and Pete, and the cowman from east of McAllister, also had their guns trained. Jason didn't; his carbine was lying loosely at his side in the rocks, and neither Doc nor Jessie had guns aimed at all, so Jason's warning about seven people being ready to fire wasn't altogether correct, but he didn't know that.

Neither did those three nightriders sitting up there like graven images cast in neutral, dusty stone. Even their tuckered horses didn't move. Frank Hall had that one with the bandaged arm drawn right down his rifle barrel through the rear sight. He curled his finger and breathed very shallowly. There was no mistaking the grim intentness of either Frank or Jess Palmer. They'd shoot at the bat of an eyelid, and they'd shoot to kill.

The foremost outlaw let his breath out. His shoulders drooped. It didn't make any difference to him whether there were seven guns down there blocking his route, or seventy; all it took to kill a man at this close range was good aim and one curled finger. He very slowly turned his head. The others looked stricken; they gazed at the foremost man a full ten seconds before the injured one said in a reedy, tired tone of voice: 'All right, Mack; it's over. We done our damndest an' it's over.'

Mack slackened his reins, glanced forward a moment then huskily said, 'All right, Weatherell; you win. I'm goin' to get down.'

Frank started to say something about that. He started to raise up, but the one called Mack was already jack-knifing out of the saddle. Frank watched and had his lips parted to speak, but didn't say a word.

Jessica turned and looked at Doc as though to tell him he'd been wrong, that those men were worn out from running and had no fight left in them. She never got it said, except for the eloquent look.

The other two outlaws also started to dismount. They were as stiff and bone-weary as their spokesman also was, judging from their sluggish, dusty, leaned-down matter of moving. Randy muttered something in a tone of calm disgust and lifted his shoulders and head, turning to look around at Frank and Jess. Pete Pierson moved also, but Pete struck some stone-chips underfoot and paused to get a better purchase before arising.

That foremost outlaw up there on the ridge tugged his horse and started moving down towards the rockfield. He hadn't covered twenty feet when his head-hung animal trudged on up beside him. That was when the nightrider made his play. All the outward lassitude vanished in a second. He took two fast, wide steps and got on the far side of his horse. The other two did the same thing and they were farther back so they made it even smoother. A gun bucked and roared from around on the far side of that leg-weary lead-horse. Randy gave a little cry and flopped against his rock, slid down it out of sight just as Frank drove a shot at the foremost outlaw's hat, visible over the seating-leather of his saddle. The bullet missed.

The other two nightriders opened up with pistols, too, driving lead into the rocks and forcing everyone, even furious Frank Hall, down behind the stone cover. Jason cried out in a searing voice at the outlaws. They swung their guns and made Jason get belly-down also.

Doc pushed his carbine between the cleft where he lay, wiggled lower to get the weapon seated against his shoulder, and tried to bend far enough to his right to swing the gun southward to bear. He couldn't; the cleft was too narrow. With an angry curse he jerked the gun clear and started to raise up. Two slugs struck his protective stone high up, showering Doc with razor-fine particles of sandstone and granite. He involuntarily flinched.

Jessica pushed her little Colt Lightning six-shooter out and fired three shots up the hill. Someone slammed a big .45 slug against her rock too, forcing her back down and away from the soft curve of her particular stone shield.

Pete Pierson didn't get off a shot. He was closest to Randy, and crouched there through the ranging gunfire staring in total disbelief at a dead man.

Doc heard horses running and risked raising up. The nightriders were racing frantically back the way they'd come, eastward. But they each rode twisted from the waist to fire, and a bullet sang uncomfortably close to Doc's head, making him drop down again.

Frank Hall jumped straight up white in the face, his eyes ablaze, and fired his carbine empty at the fleeing men. He missed every time, not because Frank was any worse rifle shot than any of the others, but because the way those renegades rode they made extremely difficult targets even from a standing position.

Jason bawled for someone to get their horses. He was like a bearded prophet from ancient times, jumping up and wildly gesturing to the others. 'Save your bullets! Never mind tryin' to hit them now! Get to horseback; we've got better animals. We'll run them down.'

Doc stepped over and helped Jessica to her feet. The pair of them stood a moment looking far out beyond carbine range where the desperadoes were cruelly spurring their tired, tucked-up mounts in a wild and frantic attempt to get away.

Frank and Jess went after their animals. Jason started after his horse, too, then he came even with Pete and Randy and halted. Pete looked up at him. 'He's dead,' he said. 'I don't believe it—but it's true. That bullet hit him right through the head. They killed him, Jason.'

CHAPTER ELEVEN

By the time the others were mounted to ride Doc was just finishing an examination of Randy. He shook his head as Frank Hall rode up leading Doc's horse.

'Hardly had time to realise what'd happened to him,' Doc said, and glanced around as the others came up to him, their carbines fisted, their faces locked down in cold fury. 'Hey,' he said softly to them all. 'You're not going to leave him lying here in these rocks while we go chase those nightriders, are you?'

Frank Hall looked past where Jess Palmer was walking up leading two horses, his own and the dead man's mount. Frank said, 'Give Jess a hand, Doc. You fellers lash him across his horse.' Frank turned and jerked his head at Pete and Jason. 'Let's go,' he growled, and booted his horse out through the rocks towards the meadow beyond where they'd all have a clear run after the escaping killers.

Jess grunted as he and Doc Heatly boosted the limp corpse up, belly-down across the dead man's own saddle. Jessica lingered with them. When they'd wordlessly, grimly, completed the tying and lashing Jess said, 'Jessica; you can take him down to town. We can't haul him where-ever this here chase is goin' to take us. An' he's got a wife down there. She ought to have the say where he's to be buried.'

Jessica looked across the dead man over at Doc. He nodded back at her. 'You can make it all right. Go back the way we got up here and swing southward the first pass you come . . .'

'I know how to get down there,' she broke in to say to Doc. 'Only; I think I ought to go with you, George. You and my father and the others.'

He shook his head at her again, saying, 'No, Jessica; do as I say. Take him back to his wife. Then wait for us down in town. I'll feel a lot better that way.' He turned to gaze out where her father, Frank and Jess, were dusting it swiftly on the trail of the renegades. 'It'll be better all round if you're not along, Jessica.' He was thinking they'd corner those men somewhere back in the yonder wilds and if she wasn't along to see how hard men sometimes died, it would be better for her, for him, for all of them.

Old Jess got astride and leaned to hand Jessica the reins of Randy's horse. 'Honey,'

106

he told her. 'You go on an' do as Doc says. It's for the best. We'll get back to town by mornin', maybe, and then you can join your paw.' He smiled into her wide and greeny eyes. 'Like Doc says; a man wouldn't feel right, you maybe gettin' hurt an' all.' He pushed the reins into her hand, straightened up, saw those two younger people looking straight at one another, then urged his horse between them over closer to Doc. 'Let's go,' he muttered, 'Or we'll lose 'em out there.'

'Don't fret,' Doc said to her, and let his horse follow Palmer's animal out through the boulder field. She called after him softly.

'Be careful, George.'

Jess raised his mount to a high lope when he was able, and went rocketing along in the wake of the others. Doc came swiftly along behind him. Once, he turned in his saddle and waved. After that he concentrated on what lay ahead.

The chase out there had gone over against the westerly sagebrush hills, then had turned north as the renegades sped along, wisely keeping a dusty sidehill always on their off side so they couldn't be easily discerned. It wasn't actually much help, but they had a good lead and didn't need much more speckled backgrounding than they got.

Jason, Frank, and Pete Pierson were a good mile behind. They'd closed some distance by swerving across the meadow on an intercepting angle, but they were too far away and too unsteady in their saddles to attempt shooting yet, so the race was being run in full silence. If anything, this served to heighten the drama of desperation being acted out while the overhead sky reddened, the sun dropped steadily lower, and that peculiar high haziness increased as the afternoon wore along.

Jess let Doc get abreast of him and said, 'They got to keep north or cut back eastward. There's no other way for them.'

Doc hadn't been as interested in the course the fleeing men were taking as he was in the condition of their mounts. He remarked about this to Palmer, and old Jess nodded without comment as he began to shave off some of the intervening distance by swinging more and more north.

By running diagonally across the meadow Doc and Palmer were able eventually to get within shooting distance of Jason, Frank and Pete Pierson. A little later, when the renegades scudded swiftly around a fat, low hill, they actually caught up with them. Frank Hall, looking back and seeing them together again, made a sweeping gesture to his right and yelled something which Doc didn't understand, but which old Jess seemed to have no difficulty at all in comprehending. He called to Doc, jerked his head and cut loose from the others, heading for that fat, low hill's eastern shoulder. He led the way until Doc understood that what Frank had wanted was for the pair of them to whip around the hill over there to prevent the outlaws from doubling back.

They got around the hill, saw a little lazy cloud of dust around some trees far ahead, and, believing that dust was their prey, kept right on going. Frank, Jason and Pete, appeared to the west of them around the opposite shoulder of the low hill. Frank was frantically gesturing. Doc saw that but Jess was concentrating on the dust up there in the forest and had no inkling he was being signalled to until Heatly yelled his name and pointed. Then old Jess looked, and frowned, and swung his head back and forth. He didn't understand what Frank was so frantically trying to tell them with his arm motions either.

It was Jason who got the idea communicated to them. He slid his big horse to a hard halt, lifted his carbine and fired up the hill. Doc and Jess turned. They saw dirt fly where Jason's slug had hit. Then, belatedly, they saw something else; dust up there on the ridge of the fat hill where riders had run up there, topped out, then had plunged down the far side back into the rearward meadow.

'They doubled back,' yelled old Jess, fighting his excited horse around. He swore lustily at the top of his voice as he completed his half-acre turn. Doc's horse had a better rein, but also, he slowed it considerably before turning. Over across the width of the fat hill, Frank and his companions were also coming about.

Doc forgot about that dust cloud up there in the trees. Whatever had caused it, a startled buck, maybe a prowling bear searching for bee-trees, or anything at all, it was not made by the three nightriders. They had sagaciously saved their animals, and perhaps their necks as well, by cutting sharply along the far side of the low, fat hill, before their pursuers had sighted them. Then had ridden straight up there, across the top while their pursuers were racing around both shoulders of the hill, and then straight down the far side back into the meadow again.

It was a slick move. As he rolled along to the rough gait of his borrowed animal he had to admire the sly, coldly calculating nerve of those killers. Then he suddenly thought of Jessica. She'd taken that same trail leading down through the stonefield, down through that jumbled pass out of the highlands!

He spurred his horse. It ran ahead of Palmer in a wild rush of speed. Old Jess looked around, then bent low and hooked his horse too. The others didn't get back down into the broad meadow until Doc was half way across it riding like a madman. The outlaws were small and growing smaller. They'd gained more time by tricking their pursuers. They weren't wasting a second of it either; men in their boots, riding animals as nearly finished as their animals were, had to strain every resource and rely on every tactic, just to stay alive. They were doing it.

Doc was well out front when he saw the nightriders swerve close out there, coming all together, as they headed in a straight line straight into the boulderfield, down the clearly marked trail of the pass over there, then, as the ground dropped away, they sank from his sight.

Somewhere far back and over where Frank, Pierson and Jason Weatherell were hastening to converge on Jess and Doc, a man cried out a wild warning. Doc didn't heed it; he had his carbine in his right hand, up and ready to be used one-handed. The uppermost thought in his mind was Jessica; he had to divert those nightriders before they came onto her down the trail somewhere.

He knew, as he raced closer to the pass, that she'd had a good lead, but he also knew that she wouldn't be expecting the nightriders to come charging down behind her. His thoughts concerning a meeting down there somewhere, chilled his blood. She had two good horses with her. Men who'd deliberately murder a total stranger—Fred Coffey—just because they thought he was getting too close to them, wouldn't hesitate a second to kill a girl, if she offered salvation for at least two of them, with those horses she was travelling with.

That booming, loud cry of warning sounded again. That time Doc turned his head. Jess was a hundred yards farther back. Frank, Jason and Pete were closing fast on old Jess, coming diagonally across the meadow. Doc turned forward, shot past the first outlying boulders and a gun roared ahead of him to one side of the trail. His mount shied violently. Doc lost his hat and one stirrup. He had to make a frantic grab for the mane to keep from also losing his other stirrup and the saddle as well. He tried to stop the horse. It kept on charging, either stung by that bullet or simply running away with Doc.

He got sufficiently straight in the saddle to use both hands on the reins, and finally the horse slowed. But another shot came, and that time the horse shuddered under Doc, gave a stumbling lunge, and fell. He went off sideways, reacting instantly and instinctively to the fall. He landed on his feet but momentum dumped him headlong. Fortunately he didn't strike any of those large rocks head-on, but he did slam up against a loose rock that gave a little under the impact, and finally all sense of movement ceased for him.

He tried to sit up and toppled over. He tried again and made it that time, with a quick stab of pain down his right side from his upper arm and shoulders where he'd struck the rock. The third gunshot crashed and roared, but now that desperate man down there in the bottle-neck of the pass was firing farther back; out where the others were wildly scattering to avoid the same thing which had happened to Doc.

Obviously, that renegade hiding down there where the pass tilted, dropped lower, wasn't trying to kill the riders; only the horses. It was sound thinking, too. Anyone set afoot up in this wild, desolate place, wouldn't be able to even reach Weatherell's ranch, let alone any of the lower-down ranches where there would be horses, for at least eight hours. That was all the time the killers would need to make good their final escape.

Doc paused to gingerly move his right arm. It pained him but it also responded, meaning nothing was broken or seriously injured. He reached down, drew forth his sixshooter and started to crawl deeper into the boulders at the side of the road.

Farther back, the others were unable to safely fire for fear of hitting Doc. He realised this when he paused once to see why the others weren't pinning down that nightrider up ahead of him somewhere in the boulders.

He told himself this looked to be a personal encounter between that killer out there and himself. He also told himself he'd neither been trained by education or environment for such an encounter. But he kept inching along nevertheless, for one basic fact was painfully clear; whether he was trained at killing or not, he did not have any alternative; if he didn't find and kill that man up ahead, not only would it very likely work in reverse with him as the victim, but also, and this was uppermost in his thoughts, Jessica was very likely to be killed when the other renegades found her.

He tried heaving rocks overhand to force his personal foe to reveal himself. The gunman didn't respond to that old trick in any way. He tried remaining prone and blocking in yards of the onward jumble for something that could be an arm, a leg, even a hatbrim. Again he was unsuccessful. Finally, he decided there was only way to conclude this deadly game, got up onto all fours and started to slip back and forth through the rocks. He hadn't covered a hundred feet when a gun blasted at him so close-by his ears rang from the thunder.

Both legs went sidewards out from under him. He felt the quick, violent surge of hot pain in one of his legs but was too desperately trying to get behind cover to heed it right then.

Another close-by shot came. This one missed his ribs by inches, but it also did something else; it permitted Doc one fleeting sighting of the rock where that ambusher was desperately trying to get him.

He knew he was hurt. He also knew this fight had to terminate fast or they'd never get down there in time to help Jessica. He also knew, if he stood up, that gunman would also expose himself to kill Doc.

He took a long breath, looked all around, saw that he was quite alone, said a little prayer to himself, got both legs under himself and started to spring upright, his sixgun cocked and swinging.

What saved him was a fluke. He was perfectly willing to wager everything on one shot each; one from his gun, one from the outlaw's gun. But it didn't work out like that at all. As he jumped up the outlaw saw him and raised up to fire. But Doc's injured leg refused to sustain him. He hadn't quite reached his full height when the leg simply dropped from under him. He started falling. He flung out an arm for support, missed the rock, saw the outlaw's contorted face and fired point-blank at it. At that same moment the outlaw also fired. He missed by two yards. Doc didn't miss at all. He shot the man directly between the eyes.

CHAPTER TWELVE

When Frank Hall came up with Jess and Jason right behind him, Doc was sitting flat on the ground. He looked up at them from where he was carefully cutting off the lower portion of his trousers to fashion a bandage, and said, 'Hunt me up a couple of fairly straight twigs, will you, Frank?' He said it so matter-of-factly that tough Frank Hall grinned at him.

'Sure, Doc. You set easy there. I'll be right back.'

Jess and Weatherell came up as Hall strode on over through the rocks to where that dead nightrider lay. They regarded Doc gravely a moment, until he said, quite sharply. 'Don't stand there. I'll be fine. Get your horses and dust it on down the pass after those other two. They'll reach Jessica. They'll kill her for the horses.'

Jason didn't move. He didn't even look concerned. He said, 'Doc; Jess didn't stay on the main trail. She was bound for McAllister, remember. Well; that McAllister trail branches off just a short way onward.' He shook his head at Doc. 'Those men couldn't even get close to her anyway. I'm not worried.'

Doc was exasperated, but as Frank came back with two halves of a shattered carbine stock, all he said was. 'How about the horses? Let's get on down-country.'

Jess and Jason turned away, hiking back where their animals were. They spoke a little back and forth as they went, which further annoyed Doc. He glared after them and told Frank they acted like they didn't want to catch those killers.

Frank said, 'Make the splint, Doc, and get hold of yourself. We all understand you were thinkin' o' Jessica when you did that damned fool stunt of gettin' a horse shot from under you. But it wasn't necessary; that's what Jason was hollerin' at you. His girl would hear those nightriders comin' for a half mile. They'd never even see her as they run on past.'

Doc worked at splinting his sprained and fractured ankle. He still felt pain in the opposite side too, from his encounter with that boulder when the horse had gone down with him. He worked efficiently and swiftly, and finally said, 'Frank; which one was he, over there in the rocks?'

'The one with the bandaged arm. He'd been shot plumb through in the fight last night down at Weatherell's place.'

'I didn't believe one of them would do it.'

'Do what, Doc?'

'Hold us off like that. Make a heroic stand while his friends ran on. Gave the others a chance for their lives.'

Frank blinked, then silently went to work creating a smoke which he afterwards pushed between Doc's lips and held a light for. 'Can you stand now?' he asked. Doc held out a hand. Frank hoisted him upwards carefully, held forth an arm for Doc to lean upon, and as Jess and Jason came back with the horses. Frank wordlessly led Doc over through the rocks where that dead nightrider lay. He

117

pointed farther down, where the trail dropped lower. There lay a dead horse down there. Both its front legs were lying at an un-natural angle to the body.

'There's your reason for him bein' a hero,' said Frank dryly. 'He wasn't tryin' to buy those other two any time, Doc. That horse broke both its front legs runnin' in the rocks, fell, and then busted its neck when it landed in the boulders. That nightrider you shot was fightin' because he was a cornered rat an' because his pardners didn't even look back, let alone turn back to try'n save him. They left him to die—and he died. That's about all there is to it. Now let's get over there and get a-horseback. It's one hell of a long way down out of here, ridin' double.'

Doc scowled. 'Frank; you'n Jess go on after them. I'll ride back behind Jason, for town.'

Frank thoughtfully led Doc over where Jess and Weatherell waited. He said, 'Forget it, Doc. We'll *all* head for McAllister.'

'Damn it,' protested Doc. 'What about Jessica? What about those lousy murderers? You can't just quit because . . .'

'Quit, Doc?' said Frank, reaching for the reins to his mount. 'I never quit on a trail like this in my life. I'm not about to quit now. But there's no longer any need to kill our horses trailing them. I reckon we know about what direction they'll take southward, so we'll head for town, get fresh-mounted, maybe pick up a man or two. Then we'll run them down. Let's go.'

Pete Pierson who was already astride and waiting, said, 'I'll stand the first two rounds at my bar when we get back.' Then he said, 'Doc; why don't you get up here behind my saddle. I'm a sight lighter'n Jason. It won't be such a burden on the horse.'

That was how they left the meadow, with a red sky behind them and a little warm breeze rustling the grass on the downward trail out of the high country. They left behind a dead outlaw and two dead horses.

Their carefully conceived ruse to take the nightriders alive had badly back-fired, through no particular fault of their own. Of course, as Doc thought privately as they were picking their way down through the wild canyon beyond that fateful meadow, if they'd simply shot first, it all would've ended back there just as they'd anticipated; with the outlaws downed, dead or at least injured. The trouble with that was simple; no matter how reasonable it was to do something like that, it didn't sit well in a man's mind, either before or after he did it.

It was one thing to ruthlessly kill nightriders in combat. It was quite another thing altogether to give them no more chance than they gave others. A man couldn't justify vengeance against desperadoes if he became like them to exact his vengeance.

119

It was one of the peculiar things in life, Doc thought, then had his thoughts rudely brought back to the immediate present by the far-away sound of a gunshot. 'Good gawd,' he murmured, raising up behind Pierson. 'Jessica!'

Jason turned his bearded face and gazed at Doc a moment, before shaking his head. But he didn't say anything. Neither did the others. Doc didn't understand for several hundred yards why Jason had shaken his head, but where two old sentinel juniper trees stood, shaggy and smelly, Jason swung down, walked ahead, got down on one knee in the increasing dusk and made a long, painstaking study. Doc and the others didn't actually make out the trail that twisted away beyond those two trees until they were right up there within twenty feet of it.

Jason stood up, dusted his knee, looked around and said, 'This is where she turned off. There are her marks. The others, when they got down here, kept right on running southward. I doubt if they even saw this trail.'

Then, Doc understood why Jason had been so positive it hadn't been Jessica that mysterious, solitary gunshot had been directed at. He and the others resumed their downhill course, being careful as the gloom heightened around them throughout the wild hills and canyons. Frank Hall eventually said in a lowered voice, 'Some damned unlucky cowboy, probably,' without adding to it that he meant perhaps some rangerider had stumbled onto the fleeing nightriders, and had been shot.

Doc's leg dangled. No matter how he tried to alleviate the pain, he failed. His side and shoulder also hurt. But he rode along tolerating the discomfort, his thoughts on ahead somewhere. Night began closing down. The last flash of red sunlight made a big, silent explosion out over the roof of the world, then that scarlet disc slipped from sight. Shadows thickened and grew until they merged into a soft miasma of solid greyness. There wasn't a sound anywhere. That lone gunshot had come from the southeast, in the general direction of McAllister, but only a mile or two onward through the primitive world the battered pursuers were traversing.

Jason slowed and finally held up a hand to halt the others. He sat silent for a moment, then pointed on down where tawny tan grasslands showed as a big plain which ran on farther than any of them could see. That was where the high country ended. He urged his horse forward once more, and because the trail narrowed between two sheer, brushy shoulders, he took the lead while the others rode one behind the other. Doc and Pete were last in line. They could see nothing at all but Jess Palmer directly in front of them until the narrow draw began to gradually widen. It ended where the last hillsides fell away and the prairie came up to meet them.

Jason stopped again, holding them all up, until he was satisfied it was safe to emerge upon the plain, then they cut easterly and rode a hundred yards before they saw a head-hung horse, drooping and straddle-legged, out there a short distance ahead. Beyond the horse tumbled and lifeless as they'd more or less expected, was a dead man lying face-down in the cured grass.

They got down, all but Doc, paced on up, ignored the worn-out horse and gazed at the man. Doc could see him plainly. His sixgun still had its tie-down over the hammer. The cowboy had been killed before he even had a chance to yank loose his safety-leather.

'One shot,' said Jason, straightening up from a brief look. 'He must've seen them and halted to see who they were. They rode on up and one of them shot him head-on right through the brisket. He never knew what hit him.'

Frank nodded, saying, 'Get back astride, Jason. We'll send someone back from town to get this one, and that one up in the pass. Let's go.'

Jess walked over to the head-hung horse, stripped off its saddle and bridle so the animal could eat and lie down when and if it recovered from being ridden nearly to death, then they went on down-country again.

122

'Jason,' Frank Hall eventually said, his tone of voice calmly conversational. 'You still figure we got no right to hang 'em on sight?'

Jason rode nearly a hundred yards before replying. 'They deserve almost anything that happens to them,' he answered. 'But what good's the law, Frank, if, the first time men get mad, they ignore it? Lawfulness's got to start somewhere, doesn't it?'

Frank didn't answer. Doc listened to those two and looked at them. His personal feelings were with Frank, but his honest conviction lay with Jason. The trouble was, as he told himself, a man was no lofty saint atop a mountain; he was a raw-natured animal in a world of vicious other raw-natured animals, and while it was good to think lofty thoughts, it was also very practical to stamp out evil the surest and swiftest way.

There was no such thing as peace, for example; there never had been. Peace, either in this context of two murderous nightriders running for their lives and savagely killing anyone who got in their way, or in the context of disciplined marching armies, was one of mankind's loftiest illusions. Practically, there had never in all history been true peace, and there never would be, simply because man was not a docile animal any more than a bear or a wolf was a docile animal. Man would have to change completely, even down to his habit of eating meat, to even come close to being a peaceful animal, and Doc had no illusions this would ever happen.

Men like Jason Weatherell who lived apart with their pure dreams of a better world didn't belong down where men struggled hardest for the things all men held dear. They didn't belong for the elemental reason that they were deluded about mankind. They thought men could change, and no one could deny that man *should* change. But the elemental fact was undeniable: Man would never change! All the old ways of violence were ancient and predictable; they were unchanging and that was all there was to it.

Then Frank said something that made Doc study him for a minute after he'd said it. He looked across at Jason and softly smiled. 'Everybody believes in what's right, Jason,' he quietly said. 'It's just that nobody ever practises it.'

Pete and Jess were also listening, but like Doc, they had no views of their own to offer. Doc knew why that was; they felt as he also felt. They liked what Jason stood for; even admired it. But they behaved as Frank Hall behaved. If they could get a bead on those two surviving killers running scairt ahead of them somewhere in the night, they'd kill them without a second thought.

That's how it was. That's how it always had been. That's how it would continue to be, and all the Jason Weatherells in the world were never going to change it one bit.

They came within sight of McAllister shortly after Frank made that remark to old Jason, so nothing more was said for a while. It was a relief to each of them, but particularly to Doc who was in constant agony, to realise that they were out of the wild high country and down to civilisation again.

Pete Pierson said, 'I sure need a drink.'

Jess muttered agreement to this under his breath. Frank and Jason rode along saying nothing, just gazing ahead at the lights.

CHAPTER THIRTEEN

Jessica had arrived in McAllister only a short while ahead of the others. She was, in fact, still at the hotel hitchrack with the two horses, when her father and Doc saw her. Some local townsmen had taken the dead cattleman away, but the small crowd around her was excited and shooting questions without really giving Jessica a chance to answer. When they saw Jason ride up, great beard streaked, massive bulk squared up in his saddle, the men eased away and got back upon the sidewalk behind Jessica. Some man in the crowd who knew him called over asking if they'd killed the nightriders. Old Jason fixed the man with his black-eyed look and said nothing.

Pete and Frank Hall helped Doc dismount. Until the others saw them doing that they didn't understand that Doc had been hurt. Neither did Jessica, who now moved swiftly over where Frank was supporting Doc. Frank smiled at the tall, golden girl. 'Cracked ankle,' he said quietly, 'an' a wrenched set o' side muscles. If you'll help him over to his house, Jess, the rest of us'll see about gettin' fresh horses and goin' on.'

She looked quickly upwards at Hall. 'Then—they got away, Frank?' she asked.

He nodded. 'Two of 'em did, Jess. Doc here nailed the feller with the wounded arm in the pass. It was a pretty good go-round. Remind me someday to tell you about it. Doc did right good.'

Frank started to turn as Jason and Jess came up. Pete Pierson had disappeared the moment they hit the edge of town. Frank started to say something about securing fresh mounts, but Doc cut across his sentence.

'I'm not out of this,' he said to Frank Hall. 'I'll go the rest of the way in a livery rig.'

Frank paused in his talk, steadily regarded Doc a moment, then hoarsely chuckled. 'No, Doc; you stay back this time. I plumb admire your grit, you understand, but . . . in a buggy, Doc . . .?'

Jessica suddenly said, 'Why not, Frank? From here on, if they went south or west, it's all flat country for a hundred miles.'

Jason suddenly fell to combing his beard with a set of bent fingers. 'Frank,' he said, catching Hall's attention. 'She's right. And he's earned the right.'

Hall blinked incredulously at old Jason. 'In a top-buggy,' he protested, 'chasing nightriders, Jason? I never heard o' such a thing.'

Jason agreed with that. 'Neither have I, Frank, but then up until a few years back I'd never heard of a rifle that'd shoot more'n one slug o' lead at a time either.' He looked past where his daughter was helping Doc stand. 'Go get the rig,' he told her in that deep-down, drum-roll voice of his, and no one said any more one way or another.

Two cowmen from the eastern ranges stepped up in front of Jess Palmer. Both were gravely serious. 'We're ready to go along,' they said. Jess nodded, told them to fetch their horses, and was turning to join Jason and Frank as they struck out for the liverybarn, when Pete Pierson came loping up with a shiny bottle of amber liquor in each hand.

'Supper,' he called out. 'Hey; wait up. I brought along some supper.'

The crowd started following, loudly talking, some of the men even hooting and laughing. They were near the liverybarn entrance when Frank turned on them. 'What's so funny?' he snarled. 'Fred Coffey's dead. Randy Collins is dead. There's a cowboy dead out a few miles

127

below that pass up into the high country, and farther up where that pass breaks over into a big meadow, there's a dead nightrider. Damned if I find anything to laugh about in that.'

The crowd went silent. Back beyond the first row Agnes Carlisle was shoving her way through. She had a plaid tablecloth wrapped into a bundle in both hands. When she got through she said, 'Here; one of you take this. It's food.'

Old Jess took it and smiled at her. 'Thanks, ma'am. Your cookin' is what'll make all the difference.'

She said, 'Don't bring them back. I mean the men who killed Fred Coffey.'

Dave Miller the liveryman was hobbling around and bellowing orders at a swamper while they both feverishly worked at rigging out fresh animals. Dave told Jason he'd go along too. Jason looked down at Dave's cane and back up again. He didn't refuse, he simply shook his head and shouldered on past. Next, Dave went up to Frank. Hall was blunt.

'Not a chance, Dave. We don't need any more men; what we need is fast horses an' to get goin'. We're wastin' good time here in town.'

'But hell,' protested Miller. 'Doc's goin' in a rig. I could do the . . .'

'Forget it, dammit,' exclaimed Frank Hall, his patience getting out of hand for a second.

'Just help us get fresh animals.'

Someone came across the road holding aloft a lantern. It was Carey Holdorf, the paunchy storekeeper. No one paid any attention to Carey although they were grateful for the light he held up.

Jessica helped harness a horse to a yellow-wheeled runabout, while Doc and Pete Pierson stepped over into a dark tie-stall and each had a stiff jolt of Pete's whiskey. Outside, the crowd made a low, continuous sound as those people out there talked and speculated. Jason and Frank were already mounted. Jess was toeing in to mount up and those two cattlemen who'd volunteered to go along were coming across the road on their private animals when John Fleming the parson said loudly from the forefront of the crowd where he'd pushed his way through, 'The good right arm o' the Lord'll be with, gentlemen. You'll be His instruments in this night's work.'

Old Jason's head jerked up, his black eyes sought out Parson Fleming. He stared hard and was on the verge of speaking when Doc and Jessica, from the seat of their runabout, called over.

'Clear the doorway, please.'

They drove out and turned southward. Something about the indomitable will of those two, a handsome girl and an injured but determined man, made several men in the crowd yell out strong encouragement.

129

The entire crowd took it up, waving encouragement as Jessica drove straight down towards the southern end of McAllister.

Frank Hall rode out next, then Jason and Pete and Jess Palmer. The last two horsemen were those volunteer cowmen. They were the only ones who looked fresh and alert; all the others looked, and were, weary, saddle-sore, and gaunt.

They favoured their animals as far as the end of town to warm them out of any stiffness from standing in stalls they might have, then, where the plain came up, they eased them over into a long lope and cut westerly out over the prairie. It was, as someone back in town told Aggie Carlisle, the damndest looking posse he'd ever seen in all his borned days; Doc Heatly with half of one trouser leg cut off to hold a splint to his injured leg, that splint being made of the two halves of a carbine stock, riding in a fancy little runabout besides a beautiful 'breed girl who'd strapped two booted carbines to the dashboard of the rig, plus a bunch of hollow-eyed men who looked more dead than alive.

No one could have found fault with that description either, unless it was the possemen themselves; they could look around and except for the incongruity of Doc and Jessica and their buggy swinging and swaying along, the darkness seemed to rather well conceal all the other blemishes among them.

Fresh horses made a world of difference, but when one of those two newcomers with the posse said they shouldn't have too much trouble overtaking the nightriders now, Frank Hall had a terse answer for that.

'If you think those men haven't dug up a couple of fresh animals out of someone's barn or pasture by now, you're plumb crazy.'

That dampened everyone's enthusiasm for several miles, until old Jason suddenly said, 'Stop. Stop and keep quiet an' listen.'

Everyone obeyed. They were by then about four miles south and west of town. Frank shook his head at Jason. So did Jess. But the massive, bearded mountaineer said, 'Just be quiet.'

It took nearly a full two minutes, and afterwards everyone but Jessica was astonished that Jason had picked up those sounds so much earlier than the others, but eventually they heard them: Ridden horses far off westerly in the night, passing straight southward in a hurry.

Frank turned. 'You boys,' he said to the pair of cowmen who'd joined them at town. 'Get on down-country as fast as you can make it, and cut over in front of 'em if you can. Be damned careful; they've already killed some danged good men. Try and hold them; or at least try an' turn em' towards the rest of us.'

The cattlemen nodded, spun out their horses and loped from sight. Jess, who was watching them go, winced noticeably when one of their horses struck hard granite with his shod hooves. 'They'll hear that for sure,' he told Jason and Frank.

Frank muttered, 'Let'em. Come along now.' The entire cavalcade opened up their animals and bore steadily towards those nightriders out there.

Jessica handled the lines to the buggy while Doc sat back trying to cushion his sore body and badly swollen ankle from the jolts. He wasn't often successful; Jess tried her best but in the darkness pot-holes and old buffalo wallows had a habit of appearing deceptively flat, until the front wheels fell into them.

Still, Doc and Jessica had the best of it; at least they had springs under them. Moreover, each time Jessica hit a chuck-hole she'd lean over, her arm and shoulder rubbing close to Doc, and apologise. Doc liked it; it almost made him forget his aches.

Eventually Jason slowed and signalled for the others to do the same. He went along after that trying to catch more sounds, but the party with him made too much noise so in the end he called another of those still halts. But now he, nor the others, could hear anything at all. Jason grunted, shifted his weight in the saddle and said, 'They heard us. They've cut straight west.'

Frank slashed the air with his right arm pointing out the new course. All of them hastened onward again. Once, Jess said, 'Hell, Frank; they got to be over on my range.'

Frank's answer was curt. 'But not for long, Jess. Not at the rate they're movin', an' not for long, now that they know we're back here givin' chase.'

Jess thought a while then suddenly straightened in his saddle with a loud groan. 'They'll have got a couple of my horses sure as the devil. I left two of my best animals in the barn!'

No one commented about that. For another mile they simply sped along. Doc looked southward and Jessica, anticipating his thoughts, said she too wondered where those two cattlemen were, down there.

When their mounts began to hang heavily in their bits, they were forced to slacken off to give them a 'breather.' This afforded everyone, but mostly Doc Heatly, a chance to relax frayed nerves and muscles. Overhead, a thickening kind of pale fogginess clouded over the moon and stars. Frank cocked an eye at it. So did Jason and Jess. Pete was over on the far side of the buggy leaning down surreptitiously pushing something in at Doc. In a stage whisper he said, 'Medicine, Doc. Best kind medicine for achin' sprains, black an' blue ribs. Take a jolt.'

Doc did. He'd have taken two jolts but Jessica reached out, took a firm hold of the bottle and insistently tugged. He surrendered it reluctantly and she handed it back to Pete with a cold, forbidding stare. Pierson smiled a little uneasily and stowed his bottle back in his saddle pockets just as Frank Hall said, 'It'll be rainin' by dawn, is my guess, an' if that does anything, it'll blur their tracks.'

Jason stroked his beard and said nothing, but obviously he was thinking some hard and realistic thoughts, for a mile further when they were ready to lope again, he studied that hazy, high, warm sky and said, 'I don't think so, Frank. I think the Injun summer's goin' to end though; maybe tomorrow, maybe the day after. Then we'll get a killing frost at the very least. But it'd have to stay warm for it to rain.'

Pete Pierson was annoyed by this calm speculation over the weather. 'What's the difference?' he called over to the others from his position near the buggy. 'What matters is how much time we can make tonight, isn't it?'

No one answered him. Southward and westward, a sudden quick burst of far-away gunfire erupted. Every one of them yanked straight up and whipped around facing that direction.

'Them boys who joined us in town,' shrilled old Jess Palmer.

No one disputed this. As though given an invisible fresh direction they all turned and spurred up their horses into a run, heading straight down towards that sound. There were several more shots, but ragged now, irregular

134

and sounding from totally different directions.

Doc told Jessica he thought the cowmen had either ambushed the nightriders, or else it had happened the other way around. But that in either event one pair had gotten first look and had opened with everything they had.

That seemed about right. But even in a speeding buggy with springs and a tufted leather seat, it was impossible to carry on much of a conversation, so Jessica didn't attempt to answer. She had to try and anticipate the bumps. Doc finally lay a hand upon her arm and told her to get in behind the horsemen; that by watching them, she'd know what lay immediately ahead. She did it, and at once they had easier going.

There were no more shots down there, so after a mile of running, the possemen had to slow their animals in order to be certain they were heading in the correct direction.

They were; they found that they were when a riderless horse threw up its head and violently shied as they came racing on up. Jason made a lunge towards the beast and it eluded him, darting away into the westerly darkness. 'Fan out,' cried Jason. 'Whoever he was, he's got to be around here somewhere; hurt or well, he's on foot.'

It was Pete Pierson who found that riderless horse's master. It was one of the cattlemen and he was leaning bent over using his carbine to support himself. When Pete yelled the others

135

converged. Doc started to jump out to go help the man, but Jessica restrained him. Frank and the others got down though.

The cowman had lost his hat. He seemed more dazed than injured. As he recognized the possemen he straightened up a little and made a weak, southerly gesture. 'That way,' he said unsteadily. 'They must've heard us. We didn't even see 'em until one of 'em let fly straight between us. Then all hell busted loose.'

Jason suddenly said, 'Quiet! A rider's coming!'

Everyone reached for a weapon, but when the rider appeared it was the other cowman. He ignored the guns pointed at him and said, 'How's Slick? Did they get him?' The dazed man looked around.

'Didn't get me, but they sure knocked the wind out o' me.'

Frank turned brusque. 'We're close,' he snapped, heading back for his horse. 'You,' he said to the mounted cowman. 'Help your pardner catch his horse then take him on back to town an' see that his hurt is cared for.' Hall flagged forward. 'The rest of you—let's go!'

CHAPTER FOURTEEN

Doc told Jessica as they moved out southward behind the others, that this was the second

136

time now in their chase of the nightriders that the same few had ended up still going while reinforcements had been knocked out of the fight.

She nodded, driving with her head raised slightly to watch the horsemen up ahead who were trotting now, no longer rushing headlong, because clearly, wherever those outlaws were down here, they'd amply demonstrated that they were neither novices nor cowards; they were consummate bushwhackers. No man in his right mind rode into an ambush, even when it was commanded by only two men.

Frank Hall called a halt after a while. They came all together. He said, 'I don't like this. We can't hear 'em or see 'em, an' furthermore ridin' all bunched up like we've been doin' is sort of inviting them to drygulch the lot of us.'

Old Jess kept looking uneasily around. 'I'd just like to know where they went, is all,' he said. 'After all, they didn't hardly have that big a start on us, back there.'

Jason, who'd been stroking his beard in deep thought, said, 'I wouldn't be plumb surprised if they turned about an' went right through us, back northward. Boys; I don't know them at all, but I've seen an' heard enough tonight to feel convinced they're mighty sly renegades.'

Pete Pierson passed one of his bottles around. Jason let it go by but everyone else had a pull on the bottle. Doc accepted it from Pete and also had a drink. Jessica watched soberly, and when Doc wasn't looking she threw a withering glare out at Pete. After he retrieved his bottle he rode farther away from the rig.

'No point in this ridin' along with nothing to guide us,' said Frank. 'Pete; you an' I'll look southward. Jason; you see if they really did slip around us an' go back into the high country. Jess; you'n Doc an' Jessica spread out an' look to the west.'

Palmer said, 'Frank; that don't leave anyone to scout to the east.'

Hall nodded. 'You're right. Well; I'll sashay over in that direction, and Pete can scout southward alone. How's that?'

No one objected, so they began breaking up, each of them spreading out. Jess Palmer told Doc he'd cut northwest, which would leave the southwesterly country for Doc and Jessica to scout through.

None of them rode fast now; none of them was certain they wouldn't stumble into an ambush, for one thing was abundantly clear to each of them: Wherever those surviving nightriders were, north, south, east or west, they weren't so far ahead that their hoof-falls couldn't be heard. And yet—no one could hear them.

'Playing the coyote's game,' Jessica told Doc. 'Walk along carefully for a hundred

138

yards, then stop and wait to hear someone coming after you.'

'Pleasant thought,' murmured Doc, reaching forward to tug out a carbine and hold it across his lap. 'And we're sitting up here in this buggy like two clay pigeons at a shooting gallery.'

'We could stop a moment,' she said.

Doc looked at her. 'What good would that do?'

'Well; probably none as far as the nightriders are concerned, George,' she said, slowly smiling at him.

He grinned. 'I'm a little slow tonight,' he said, reaching to touch her.

'That's all right,' she said. 'I like my men strong as oak and twice as thick.'

He laughed and she kissed him squarely on the mouth. Then, when he reached out, she ducked away and flicked the lines making their harness animal break over into a choppy trot. Doc gasped as the two off wheels bounced into and out of a chuck-hole, grabbed for the seat-railing and said, 'All right, all right. You got your point across. We're manhunting.'

Old Palmer jogged in once or twice to squint through the gloom, evidently reassuring himself they were still close by, then went back out and southward again. The last time he did that he called softly, saying this was all a wild goose chase; that those killers wouldn't

139

head west, they'd keep travelling southward.

Doc didn't answer. Neither did Jessica, but when old Palmer had gone again she said, 'If they did go west, and if Uncle Jess keeps making all that noise out there, they'll hear us long before we even get close to them.'

Doc said nothing about that, but he fell to thinking back to when they'd first headed into the uplands with old Jess and Frank Hall leading them. 'You know, Jessica, when we were riding up into the high country towards your place, and only Frank and Palmer knew you folks lived back in there, neither one of them told the rest of us a thing. They were taking us straight to your paw's house across his land, and never once did they let the rest of us know that they even knew anyone lived back there at all.'

'My father has always liked it like that, George,' she explained. 'He's never exactly made a secret of the fact that we were back there. But he's asked Frank and Uncle Jess and some of the other cowmen who occasionally pass through, not to make a point of talking about us or our ranch.' She looked around a little anxiously. 'I don't suppose that makes much sense to you, George, but after my mother died, and after a few other unpleasant things happened to my father, he just withdrew from the world.'

Doc nodded. He'd noticed that withdrawal the day before, and even earlier than that, for a fact. He did not share old Jason's sentiments entirely, nor could he have been expected to because they lived in different worlds, but Doc was a thoughtful, tolerant man; he could at least understand why Jason was as he very definitely was and a man who understands another man rarely condemns him. At least he doesn't if he has the depth-perception and the basic comprehension which makes it possible for wise men to smile at those who differ from them, without also judging them.

'You think he's odd, don't you?' Jessica suddenly asked, apparently misinterpreting Doc's long silence.

He looked down at her. 'Not odd, Jessica. But all men can't live as Jason lives. Even if they could I doubt if most of them would want to. Being alone, apart, cut off, requires a special breed of folks; resourceful, strongly confident and capable.' He shook his head. 'Everyone has some particular adaptability, Jessica, but very few men in this world have the knack for completely looking after themselves.'

She heard him out then relaxed back against the seat. 'You put it very well,' she murmured.

They passed along through the pewter gloom without any sign of Jess Palmer for a long while. Because they were not pushing the harness-horse they didn't actually cover a lot of ground, although time ran on making it seem that they'd put several miles behind them. Doc tried to make out buildings off on their right, northward, and failed. When Jessica asked him what he was looking for, he told her the Palmer ranch was off there some place.

She said, 'It's farther north.' Then she said, 'I've been thinking, George. Every time someone's run onto those renegades, it's ended up badly. Maybe we ought to turn a little southward and keep Uncle Jess in sight.'

He didn't reply. He didn't get the chance. Up ahead a low, cautious whistle rang out. It was off to his right. The last time they'd seen old Jess, he'd been well southward of them, or on their left. Doc reached for the lines ahead of where Jessica was holding them and gently eased back.

'Quiet,' he whispered to her, and leaned forward to climb down with his carbine in hand. Pain mushroomed up through him the second his puffed-up lower leg came in contact with the ground. He stifled a gasp, ground down his teeth, let a second or two go by, then felt his way up along to the harness-horse's head. He raised a hand to stroke the beast's nostrils, then let the hand lie there inches above the animal's nose, ready in a second to cut off any sound the horse might try to make if it caught the scent of other horses.

Jessica came along on the opposite side to the horse's head. She also had a carbine. He shook his head at her, warning her to be absolutely silent. She understood.

For what seemed an eternity of time, nothing happened. There wasn't another sound out there. Doc was certain of one thing: Whether those men were actually trying to waylay them or not, on westerly where the night was darkest, he wasn't going to take Jessica one step further until he knew who, and what, was awaiting them up ahead.

She put her lips close to his cheek and said, 'They heard the buggy coming. They probably think it's some rancher returning home late from town.'

He nodded. 'You stay right here. I'll go out a short ways and have a look.'

She stiffened with one hand partially raised, as though to restrain him, but he limped away and she didn't reach out. She put her fingers to her throat and intently watched for as long as Doc was in sight.

That low, melancholy whistle came again. This time it seemed to be southward and perhaps slightly closer to the buggy. Doc halted, twisted slightly and concentrated on this new direction, then, a foot at a time, started stalking the man down there who'd made that sound, that signal to his pardner. Doc was confident that he and Jessica had stumbled upon the killers. He also knew that one gunshot would bring the others in a dead run to this place, but he made no move to fire such a shot. He wanted these nightriders killed or caught. He didn't want them frightened away.

A second low, soft whistling sound came from behind Doc, approximately back where he'd left Jessica with the rig. He at once swung around and started rapidly limping back. It sounded to him as though those nightriders were closing in.

He got almost back to the rig. In fact he could see its outline on ahead, with Jessica standing near the horse's head, when off to one side a man's deadly voice said in a very silky, lethal way, 'That's far enough mister. Steady now, right where you are!'

Doc's heart slammed up and down making his breathing difficult. The man was out of his line of vision, but beyond any question Doc was well limned in the unseen man's sights. To try whipping around to fire would be fatal. That voice hadn't sounded more than sixty or seventy feet off. No one, even a blind man, could miss a stationary target at that distance.

'Drop the gun, mister,' ordered that velvety voice. Doc obeyed, hoping Jessica would hear his carbine hit the earth and be alerted enough to run for it.

'Now the pistol, mister.'

Again Doc obeyed. That time, his unseen captor lifted his head and made a little chuckering sound with his lips the way grouse do. From southward and farther off an answering sound came. Doc heard his captor

144

moving in from behind. He steeled himself; those nightriders were killers, murderers. He braced for the searing, tearing sensation of a bullet.

It didn't come. In fact, it never came.

The sound of a sixgun being cocked sounded less than ten feet behind Doc. Up ahead, he saw Jessica stiffen and begin to lift her Winchester. The buggy-horse too had heard that little sound. Its ears nervously twitched.

Very quietly Doc said, 'Jess; don't do it.' He meant for Jessica not to fire. He did not believe either of them were going to live through the next five or so minutes, but he was desperately committed to a course of non-violence for as long as it could be prolonged.

The other man came in from Doc's right-hand side. He made more noise as he approached, as though, being confident and seeing his pardner controlling the situation, he could afford to take a greater chance. It was this latter man who spoke out finally, saying from a distance of perhaps thirty feet away, 'There's something wrong here, Abel. Look at this one. He wasn't like this before.'

The man directly behind Doc said. 'Never mind him, Johnny. Watch that one over yonder near the rig. He's got a gun trained this way.'

Jessica couldn't help but hear them. She said, 'And it shoots very straight.'

Doc was breathing very shallowly. His leg was sending up wave after wave of pain for him to fight against. He said, forcing his voice to be as calm as he could make it, 'If you want the buggy, boys, take it. Just leave us afoot out here.'

'Wait a minute,' the man named Abel said suddenly, his voice losing its wary softness. 'Wait just a damned minute.' He seemed startled; upset. He walked up close behind Doc and said. 'Turn around, mister.'

Doc turned. They stood three feet apart looking straight at one another. 'Doc Heatly,' gasped the man with the cocked pistol. 'Hell's bells, John; this here isn't *them*. It's Doc Heatly from town, and someone else with him.'

Doc let all his breath out. He knew that cowman standing in front of him. His name was Abel Connery. He had a combination horse and cattle outfit on the south range below McAllister. 'Mind if I pick up the carbine now?' he asked, and bent down to retrieve the weapon without waiting for an answer. He used it as a crutch, thereby taking the painful weight off his injured ankle. 'Who'd you think we were?' he asked, as the second cowman walked in for a close squint at Doc.

'Couple of fellers came onto us a mile or so south o' here and let fly,' replied the cowman. 'John an' I was headin' for home after a few

146

drinks in town. We never even seen those fellers until they dang near run right over the top of us, Doc.'

'I see. And they afterwards headed north?'

Abel lifted his shoulders and dropped them. 'Well; he don't know for sure, Doc. But we decided to hunt 'em down an' see what the hell they thought they was doing.'

CHAPTER FIFTEEN

Two shadows, one massive and thick, the other lean and light, came soundlessly out of the rearward night, both with cocked Winchesters held crossways and low. Doc saw them first. He made his voice calmly quiet as he said, 'Easy Jess. Easy Jason. These aren't the nightriders.'

Everyone turned as the two older men came in very warily, ready to shoot at the drop of a word. Abel Connery and his pardner recognized Jess Palmer straightaway, but they looked blank when huge and bearded Jason Weatherell walked up to them.

Connery said, 'Jess; what the hell . . .'

'We met back out there a piece,' explained Palmer. 'Jason swore he'd heard a couple of fellers slippin' along, so we started sneakin' in. Then we heard you talkin' to Doc an' decided to get in as close as we could before we opened up.'

Abel's pardner said something harsh under his breath and looked at Connery. 'These here fellers must be after them same two that liked to bowled us over.'

Connery didn't answer that. He said, 'Jess; who are those fellers?'

Palmer spoke as Jason was turning away. 'Nightriders. They killed Randy Collins in the high country, and another feller down on the plain. They're the ones who killed Fred Coffey. And I'll bet they've shot their way across . . .'

'Holy mackerel,' breathed the rancher standing near Doc. He slowly lifted round eyes to Connery. 'Holy mackerel, Abel, an' you said they was drunk cowhands.'

'I said *maybe* they were drunk riders, John. *Maybe.*'

Jason came back leading two horses. Without a word to anyone he handed Palmer the reins to one horse, turned and got astride the other horse. He then walked his animal on over where Jessica still stood near the rig, leaned down and spoke softly to her. She answered the same way, in a quiet, low tone. Her father straightened up and looked over one shoulder.

'Let's get to riding,' he said to old Jess.

Doc limped back and climbed into the buggy. He and Jess Palmer waved at the

148

two cowmen still standing out there, and left that place to resume their search. Doc said something to Jessica about inviting those two cowmen to join in the manhunt. She didn't answer him until they were out of sight of the rangemen, then shook her head, saying, 'George; my father said we should go southward a ways then fire a shot to bring Frank and Mister Pierson up to us.'

Doc looked surprised. 'Why?'

'Because my father also said, George, that he doesn't believe what those men told you, out there.' She swung a grave look towards him. 'They told you they were nearly run down by two horsemen who let fly at them. Did you hear any gunshots?'

Doc stared straight at her. He didn't say a word for a moment, he instead leaned out of the rig looking backward. She kept on driving until someone south and west fired a carbine. The harness-horse shied at that unexpected sound. Jessica lined him out without doing what a man would've done, without perhaps swearing at him or hitting him with the buggy whip which stood erectly in its far-side whip-socket.

Doc sat back and tried to recall what he knew about Abel Connery. The other rancher he only very vaguely recalled ever seeing around McAllister before, but Connery was an established rancher south and west of town. Doc knew that much but he didn't

149

know much more. He'd never had occasion to treat Connery for anything, and had only nodded to him a time or two. They'd shared adjoining spaces at Pete Pierson's bar; had perhaps exchanged ten sentences. That was the extent of Doc's acquaintanceship with Abel Connery except that he'd driven over Connery's range a time or two going out of town on professional calls.

Jessica halted the rig. 'Someone's coming,' she explained. Doc raised the carbine from his lap and pushed it out a little, but the converging rider proved to be Frank Hall. He'd scarcely come into view when Jess and Jason also came in out of the westerly night, and Pete Pierson came catfooting it in from the southward plain.

Frank reached the buggy first and leaned down to ask who'd fired that shot, and why. Jason halted across the harness-horse's back from Frank and said he'd signalled with that shot. Then, in his slow, rumbling, deliberate way of speaking, Jason said what he thought. Frank and the others sat their saddles listening and stonily regarding Weatherell. When he'd finished talking Doc said, 'Jess; what do you know about Connery?'

'Not a whole lot,' Palmer replied. 'He's been ranchin' hereabouts for the past four, five years. Our ranges adjoin down south a ways, but he's pretty good about seein' that his stock doesn't stray too far over into my grass. He's

150

a single man, I know, and I've worked a time or two with him separating our critters. But outside of that . . .' Jess looked around. They were all looking straight at him. 'He could've been tellin' the truth—couldn't he, boys?'

Jason reiterated in the exact wording, what Connery had said to Doc. The others weighed this in their minds. Frank Hall removed his hat, frankly perplexed. 'If we go back an' if those two aren't the ones we want, the real nightriders'll get away sure.'

'And if they *are* the nightriders, we'll be ridin' around down here all night, and never gets any closer to them than we are right now.'

'But why would local men be hiding in the hills?' asked Pierson. 'It doesn't make sense.'

'Maybe it would,' said Jason, 'if we knew why they shot Fred Coffey.'

Doc let the others argue for a while, then made a suggestion. 'All right; let's keep searching for another hour or two. We know we're close to the nightriders. If, after that length of time we don't see or hear them again, then we'll have a reasonable reason to go hunt down Connery and his pardner. Also, if those two *are* the ones, at least we'll know who we're looking for. This other way . . .'

Frank Hall said, 'Jess; you were with me in the rocks up there in the pass. If that was this Connery feller up there, how come you didn't recognize him an' say something then?'

Old Palmer screwed up his face. 'I didn't get

that good a look, Frank. Hell's bells; those fellers were up there atop a lousy ridge just barely within rifle range. Anyway; if that *was* those two, at that distance I don't see as good as I used to.'

Hall seemed doubtful about this and frowned slightly. In the end he jerked his head. 'All right. Let's do it Doc's way; let's keep pushing the search until we either find 'em or don't find 'em. If not, then let's go see those other two.' He scowled at old Jess. 'Can you find Connery's ranch?'

Jess flushed and was thankful for the darkness as he said, 'I can find it. I never have been at the house or barn, actually, but I know where they are.'

Frank jerked his head. They started riding again, spreading out as they went, making a big sweep of the southward land. In the buggy Jessica was stonily quiet until Doc asked her if she actually believed Connery and his companion were the nightriders.

'I don't know,' she replied. 'I only know that if they really were the killers, they could've shot you easily, George.'

'But they didn't, Jessica. That's what I'm driving at. They could've and they didn't.' Doc leaned back against the seat. 'I don't believe they're the men we're after.'

'Then why didn't we hear any gunshots, George? They told you they'd been shot at.'

'No, all they said was that someone had let

fly at them.'

'It's the same thing, George. They meant that they'd been fired on.'

Doc's reply was tart. 'Jess; I'd never lend a hand to hang a man because he was loose in his choice of words.'

She looked around. 'I didn't mention lynching them.'

He had a retort on the tip of his tongue, but he stifled it, held back for a moment to let his irritability pass, then in a calmer tone he said, 'For now let's just concentrate on hunting those nightriders, and for everyone's sake, I hope your paw was wrong about those two men.'

They hunted. Occasionally they sighted Frank or Pete or old Jess passing across in front of their buggy, far out. The night turned sultry. The stars became obscured by some vague, high cloudiness that seemed more haze than anything else. There was a metallic scent and taste to the air as though it might rain.

Doc looked at his watch. It was past midnight. He told Jessica the time and she nodded without looking around. He fell to studying the gloomy landforms they passed and felt slightly depressed by all this.

The second hour was almost over when up ahead someone shouted in a high, fluting fashion, bringing Doc straight up in his seat. Jessica hauled back halting the buggy. She

153

groped for the carbine she'd tucked beside her when she'd climbed back into the rig back where they'd met those two rangemen.

Another shout came, this time from off to the west, and that time at least they both recognized the voice as belonging to Jessica's father. Jason had called for them all to come over to him. Jessica started to flick the lines but Doc dropped a hand over her arm.

'Wait a minute,' he said. 'Be careful, Jess.'

Ahead of them they spotted Frank Hall moving across from east to west. Frank had his sixgun in his right hand. He didn't look up where the buggy was; he was concentrating his entire attention upon the direction from which Jason had sang out. That other man out there called again too. He seemed to be heading westward also, Jessica looked inquiringly at Doc. He removed his restraining hand and nodded.

'Go ahead. Stay within sight of Frank and go slow.'

They began moving. A rider came down to them from the north. It was Pierson. He urged his horse up and bent down to ask softly what was going on. Doc said bluntly that he had no idea, and settled his Winchester across the dashboard of the buggy.

Jessica halted, eventually, and pointed. Up ahead Frank and her father were standing beside their animals with old Jess Palmer, who was also on foot. Palmer was holding the reins of a head-hung horse.

Jessica drove right on up. Pete came in too, and slowly, stiffly, climbed down. 'What's wrong?' he inquired.

Jess looked at the horse, saying 'One of my critturs. There's m'brand on his left shoulder. I saw him staggerin' around and snuck up for a closer look.' He made an angry gesture. 'Take a look; they like to rode him to death, dang their mangy hides.'

Frank Hall turned and looked out and around. 'Good,' he growled. 'Now they're afoot out here. At least one of 'em is. But even if the other one took him up to ride double, we can catch them come sunup. No horse as used up as that other one has to be, judging from the condition of this one, can go very far or very fast, packin' double.' He looked at old Jess. 'Dump the riggin' off him,' he said. 'Turn him loose an' let's get to hunting. I think we're going to catch 'em now after all.'

Doc said, 'Frank; if it's those two back where we met them, they'd only have one horse between them.' Doc looked at Jess and Jason. 'Who saw their horses?'

Jason shook his head. So did Jess Palmer. Frank threw up both hands in strong disgust. 'You two were behind 'em. You heard them and saw them.'

'But not their horses,' stated old Jess, a trifle piqued by Frank's attitude. 'When we got up there, they was already dismounted.'

Pete Pierson suggested that they go back right now and hunt down Connery and his pardner. The others briefly mulled this, decided nothing, and Doc said, 'Frank; as you said a while back; let's get to hunting.'

They dropped the subject, waited for Jess to free the run-down horse and mount his own beast, then they scattered again, brushing the lower country both southward, eastward a ways, and also to the west.

Jessica was discouraged. She told Doc they'd been hard at it all night long and thus far had evidently been eluded or out-smarted. He attributed her demoralization to weariness and over-wrought nerves from too much tension for too long a time. He talked a little, half jokingly, to raise her spirits, and succeeded somewhat, although her smiles over at him still showed weariness.

Doc estimated the time near to dawn; perhaps an hour, an hour and a half from it, when Frank Hall and Pete Pierson met far ahead through the poor light, halted to exchange a few words, and were just moving off again when two gunshots rang out and the horses under both Pete and Frank went down like pole-axed steers, dead before they'd completed their fall.

Pete fell and rolled but Frank lit on both feet and grabbed for his booted carbine almost before his mount had stopped moving. He hurled himself down behind the horse.

Doc and the others were immobilised just for a second, the attack had come so suddenly, then everyone moved. Jessica whipped the rig around eastward heading for some flourishing, large chaparral bushes. Jason let off a bawl like a bull moose and charged off to the west. Jess Palmer was nowhere in sight, so evidently he'd been half hidden before the attack and now simply became entirely hidden.

Doc was trying to brace himself against the jolting before the buggy stopped, and at the same time raise his carbine. He didn't accomplish the latter until the former motion ceased. By then Frank Hall and Pete Pierson were blazing away into the onward patches of brush. They obviously had no idea which clump their attackers had been behind, or were now behind, but they seemed to be going on the assumption that if they threw some lead into every nearby clump they might score a hit.

One thing came of their fierce and almost immediate retaliation; their ambushers were silenced for a little while.

CHAPTER SIXTEEN

Doc gingerly got down from the buggy. Until he stood unaided beside the rig he'd had no idea just how stiff he'd become since his injuries many hours before up in that northward pass. Jessica started to also climb down, but Doc told her curtly to stay up where she was.

'Don't leave the rig,' he said. 'If we have to pull out of here fast, you have the lines in your hands.'

That wasn't his real reason for not wanting her to mix in the onward fight, but he made it sound plausible. At least Jessica nodded out at him and remained seated in the buggy.

The gunfire southward seemed to be widely scattered now, and increasingly savage. As Doc stood there, uncommitted, it occurred to him that if those nightriders out there in the brush were the same two men they'd met earlier, they'd had to move fast to get this far southward and around the possemen. The moment he thought that, he also thought of something else; it didn't make much sense, believing these men shooting at them were the same ones they'd previously met for the elemental reason that Connery and his pardner'd had every opportunity to head away from the possemen after they'd been left alone back there. No outlaws in their right mind would have willingly run this far southward, then turned back just to engage more than double their numbers in a fierce gunfight.

He put aside these speculations, finally, when he thought he knew about where his companions were, and limped forward towards the scene of the fighting. Off against the eastern horizon a pale streak of watery light showed low along the merging of sky and earth. Doc saw that but scarcely heeded it when four guns ragingly engaged each other down where Frank Hall was lying behind his dead horse.

Doc got down on one knee, when he was well within the perimeter of battle, and tried to decide where those unseen ambushers were. He didn't see them, but he saw Frank begin edging away from his horse, angling over where there was some thorny growth. Out where Hall had been the plain was open and brushed clean. Evidently Frank had noticed that paleness in the east too, and wanted to get away from the open place before it got too light for him to make it otherwise.

Doc kept watching the onward sage and chaparral, his carbine up and ready. He was a hundred or so feet behind Frank. When a bullet scuffed dust less than twenty feet from Hall, Doc drove a bullet straight into the brush clump where he thought the unseen marksman was concealed. He'd picked the wrong clump of brush; another slug struck closer to Frank. That time both of them let fly, each aiming into a different bush. One or perhaps both of them did some good, because when Frank resumed his snake-crawl away from the dead horse afterwards, no more

159

bullets came at him.

Doc saw Pierson briefly when Pete darted from one covert to another. He also thought he knew about where Jess Palmer and old Jason were hiding, but the fight was fluid; no one stayed longer in one place than it took to get off a round or two, which was the only safe way to fight under those conditions; sage and chaparral didn't turn lead. A man might be adequately concealed from sight, but he was very susceptible to probing bullets and could not therefore remain long in one place after firing.

Even Doc kept manoeuvring despite the fact that he had a strong desire not to move any more than was essential, because every time he did so, his leg and side and shoulder pained him. He got exasperated after firing one slide of his carbine empty. No matter how diligent he was in waiting to shoot at muzzleblasts through the sooty, poor light, those ambushers down there always had answering slugs, to fire straight back with. They obviously moved the instant they also fired. It was, in Doc's view, a Mexican stand-off. Their enemies out there might be out-numbered but there was no denying they were craftsmen at their murderer's trade.

Jess Palmer came over where Doc was in a crouching little run and threw himself down panting. 'We got to dislodge 'em,' he gasped, during a brief lull in the firing. 'This is no good, Doc. We got to figure some way to flush 'em out o' there like they was quail or rabbits.'

A bullet slashed brush ten feet away and Doc flinched. 'There's some difference,' he growled to Palmer. 'I never saw quail or rabbits shoot back.'

Frank Hall crept back to join Doc and Jess. He was covered with dust and was grinning like a death's-head. 'We got 'em,' he croaked. 'Just pin them down until the sun comes up, an' we can take our time at pickin' them off.'

Jess was dubious about that. 'That damned sunlight works both ways, Frank, and this underbrush don't give a man much protection.'

Doc had a suggestion to make. 'You two can navigate better than I can. Frank; you go around them to the left. Jess; you do the same on the right. I'll stay about where we are now and keep banging away to make them think we're all still up here in front of them.' As the two older men gazed at him Doc felt a little sheepish. 'It's the best I can do,' he said. 'I'm sorry.'

Hall smiled and reached out to give Doc a rough pat on the arm. 'It's good enough. 'You got enough ammunition to keep up your firing?'

Doc didn't have, so each of them left him half their carbine's bullets and several handfuls of their forty-five slugs. They then silently crawled away.

Doc watched on both sides until he couldn't see them any longer, then he got down flat, pushed his carbine around the base of his shielding bush and waited to catch gunfire again.

Evidently the ambushers had taken some encouragement from the previous fact that suddenly not so many guns were being fired over at them, because they seemed to change their pattern of shooting. Instead of laying in a fierce barrage of searching lead, they were now taking turns making calculated shots. They were, as Doc had already surmised, neither novices nor cowards. Once, they made Pete Pierson back away after he'd fired, and another time they briefly silenced Jason too.

Then Doc aimed and fired when a muzzleblast revealed where a man was concealed, and the ambushers at once realized that they didn't have just two possemen left to face after all. They both concentrated on Doc for the space of several shots, forcing a crab-crawling withdrawal which made Doc grit his teeth against the pain such a move caused him.

Jason called out to the ambushers. He had the kind of a voice which over-rode any other sounds including the crash and roll of guns.

'You can't get away, boys. You can't even stand up without being killed. You're afoot an' you're out-numbered. Make it easier for us all by just flinging out your guns.'

162

Jason's answer from the bushwhackers was a fierce volley of bullets aimed in the direction he'd called out from. For a time this silenced Jason, then he called out again from a different position. This time, his tone of voice like his words, were quite different.

'You're going to get killed. This used to be a good country for nightriders but it isn't goin' to be a good country for them any more. Unless you quit now, while you've got the chance, you're going to die out here. You've got five seconds to make up your minds.'

That time, instead of bullets, one of the killers called back. 'Hey, old whiskers; you're a long way from home. If you'd give us them damned horses when we wanted them, you'd still be home, 'an safe, an' we'd be a long way off, an' none of those fellers up there with you'd be in danger. Next time someone comes along needin' horses, whiskers, you'd best come across.'

Pierson said, 'By the time that next time happens, fellers, you'll be rottin' in your graves out here. If I was you boys I'd let the future worry about itself: I'd be worryin' about right now.'

'Count your guns,' another snarling voice answered Pete. 'Take a tally, buster. You're already shy a few men. Before we're through you'll be shy a damned sight more.'

A bullet directed towards Pierson's voice punctuated this other nightrider's statement.

It evidently didn't come very close because Pete fired, levered up and fired again, then ducked away and went scuttling through the brush to a new position.

Doc blazed away in the general direction of that last man to speak. At once the other nightrider cut loose, aiming at Doc. Jason and the others threw lead back at this nightrider, forcing him to give ground go ducking left and right through the underbrush before he could be free to shoot back again.

Doc kept it up. When his carbine ran dry he used his sixgun. When that went dry he had to re-load, but he did this swiftly, then was back in there throwing more lead. For a brief interlude Pete Pierson and Jason Weatherell didn't fire. They were craning around to see what Doc was up to. They didn't find out for the simple reason that Doc ignored them to keep firing, and as the angry nightriders out there shot back, none of the others dared crawl around through the brush to where Doc was, in order to find out.

This furious phase of the battle raged on until Doc was shot out the second time. By then Jason and Pete had surmised Heatly wasn't throwing all that lead just to be firing, so they took up, also wildly firing, when Doc had to take time out to re-load again.

Whatever the nightriders thought, one thing they knew; Doc and his companions moving around through the brush were keeping up a murderous fire. No man, regardless of wiliness or bravery, could hope to remain stationary firing back for long without being hit and perhaps killed. Both the outlaws stopped shooting. Doc worried about that the moment they stopped. Jason and Pete also slackened their gunfire, but Doc didn't, although now, his uninjured shoulder was hurting too, from the punishment it'd taken from the recoiling, bucking carbine stock.

A man's outcry rang out down where the light was beginning to tint the new day slightly. Doc paused, lowered his gun and waited. The same outcry came again, and was at once followed by a gunshot. Doc tensed. From the corner of his eyes he saw Jason and Pete raise up slightly, puzzled by all this. The next time a man's voice sounded, it was recognisably Frank Hall's angry tones spitting venom at someone out there beyond sight.

'Try it again and I'll give you a third eye,' Hall snarled at someone Doc couldn't see. 'Now drop it or I'll drop you!'

Jess snapped a similar command some little distance away. He evidently got no argument back because he said, 'That's good. Now the pistol.'

Jason raised up recklessly and Doc called over telling him to get his damned head down. Jason obeyed but Pierson didn't; Pete raised up, looked hard, then stood up. As he did that Frank Hall sang out.

'Doc; we got 'em both. They're unarmed. You fellers walk on up behind 'em, but keep your eyes open.'

Jason stood up that time, craning over at Doc. 'You all right?' he asked.

As Doc jockeyed upright using the Winchester for support, he dryly answered. 'Feel so good I'm likely to break into song.' He started hobbling in the direction of Frank Hall's earlier call. The three of them converged with the steadily firming dawn light thinning out shadows all around, brightening the slatey sky, causing a freshness to the air as well as to visibility.

Frank was standing twenty feet from the whiskery, vicious-looking leader of the nightriders. Off to his left Jess was covering the other renegade-killer. Both of them were using sixguns instead of carbines. As Jason and Pete came up, the nightriders turned to appraise them. Farther back Doc came slower and more awkwardly. The mean-eyed renegade looked longest at Doc. He seemed to derive some satisfaction from Doc's obvious battered condition. Then, as Doc came closer, the nightrider switched his gaze to look over his shoulder. Jessica was coming too, her carbine pointing straight at the whisker-stubbled, gaunt, mean-looking outlaw who was staring at her.

Jason took two long steps and reached out to tap the big outlaw, bringing his attention back around from Jessica. Jason looked both stern and unrelenting. Doc, eyeing those two, thought Jason was going to say something, but he didn't, he simply stepped back and put up his sixgun. Doc thought he understood what had happened during that slight interlude; Jason hadn't wanted to believe he'd been wrong back there, about those other two rangemen, but now, after his close-up scrutiny of the captured men, he knew that he was wrong, that neither Connery or his pardner were the killers.

Frank Hall said, 'Pete; go over 'em for hideouts. Do a real good job on this tall one. He's a sidewinder if I ever saw one.'

Pierson handed his carbine to Jess and briskly walked on up. Like the others, he assumed all the fight was gone out of their prisoners. But he'd scarcely begun to reach forth to frisk the mean-eyed man, then two corded long arms reached out, caught Pierson's throat while the other arm flashed downwards towards Pete's holstered sixgun.

It was a bad mistake on the part of the nightrider for Jason was only two strides distant. He started lunging even as the killer was reaching for Pete. Before the outlaw's hand found Pierson's holster, Jason's massive fist and arm were moving in a savage blur. He caught the renegade under the right ear with a blow that would have broken the neck and perhaps cracked the skull of a smaller man.

The outlaw's head went violently sidewards. His hat sailed away. He was spun half around by impact, then he collapsed, still holding Pete by the throat.

Pete scrambled free, jumped back and sprang upright. He was breathing hard; his eyes were murderous as he went for his pistol. Again Jason had anticipated what would happen. This time he stepped squarely across the downed man and faced Pierson, his black eyes ablaze, his wild beard awry from exertion.

'Don't draw that gun!' he rumbled at Pete. 'There's no need.'

Pierson balanced on the razor's edge of using his sixgun for a long second, then very gradually lost his tight-wound look, took his hand off the pistol butt and drew in a ragged breath as he straightened up again.

Jason turned, looking over where the nightrider Jess Palmer was covering was standing like a coiled spring, set to spring forward to help his companion, or to spring away and try running. Jason didn't say a word; he simply shook his massive head back and forth. The outlaw wilted under the black glare of massive Jason Weatherell.

Frank un-cocked his sixgun, holstered it, walked up without a word and gazed at the unconscious man. 'You hit him kind of hard,' he told Jason. 'You sure his neck didn't bust?'

Jason didn't answer but he looked worried,

until Doc limped over, knelt and bent down to examine the man lying in the churned, trodden earth. He eventually stood up again and said the man's neck wasn't broken; that he'd come around in a short while. Then he glanced over at the unhurt outlaw. That one held out both his empty hands.

'I had enough,' he croaked. 'I'm glad it's over. We ain't had anythin' to eat since yesterday afternoon. I won't give you fellers no trouble.'

'Over?' growled Frank, glaring. 'Mister; it's just beginning for you'n your friend. It's not over by a damned sight. I give you my word about that!'

CHAPTER SEVENTEEN

Frank Hall told them there weren't enough horses after he'd spoken to their captive, for them all to go on back to town. Jess glared suspiciously at the conscious nightrider.

'Where's my other horse?' he demanded.

The renegade made a pitiful gesture, holding his palms out. 'It give out on us, mister, about a mile back, right after we . . .'

'Give out!' exclaimed old Jess. 'Why, you louse, you; that was a good horse!'

'He was a good horse all right, mister,' the outlaw whined. 'But we had to sort of push

169

him, an' with him packin' double an' all . . . well . . . he just collapsed out there to the west a ways an' we tried to make a run for it on foot, then we heard you fellers comin' and had to make a stand. Mack says for us to knock the horses from under some of you fellers, then maybe we could slip aroun' and get the horses that was left. It was the only thing we had left to try.' The outlaw gazed around. 'We never figured you fellers'd stay after us like this. No posse ever done that before. Usually, they give up after a few hours of chasin'.'

'Usually,' growled Frank Hall bitterly, 'you don't kill men for nothing, like you fellers did.'

The outlaw called Mack groaned at Jason's feet. He flopped over, opened his eyes and saw massive Jason standing over him. He gave a little bleat and tried to flounder clear. Jason bent, caught the man's shirt and hauled him onto his feet. He had to hold Mack because his knees were rubbery.

'Why?' Jason rumbled. 'Why did you kill Sheriff Coffey?'

Mack put a hand up to the side of his head; for a moment or two his eyes rolled aimlessly, but eventually he could focus them. Eventually too, his legs stiffened. Jason removed his hand and stood waiting for the answer to his question.

'Coffey?' said the nightrider, his voice thick. 'We didn't know the old goat's name. Only

170

that him an' another feller come into that lousy blind canyon where we were resting the horses. If we'd known them hills better we wouldn't have had to shoot him. We didn't know that was a lousy blind canyon until it was too late. Then, we saw those two coming. Sunlight reflected off the old man's badge. We figured he somehow knew who we were. We had to shoot him.'

Doc cut in to ask who they were. That made Mack look sceptically over at Doc. 'You don't know?' he asked. Doc shook his head.

'If we knew we wouldn't be asking,' he retorted. 'Who are you?'

Mack seemed to consider this a moment then all he said was, 'What's the difference; you got us; for knockin' off that old man with the badge you'll lynch us anyway. So what difference does it make who we are?'

Pete Pierson said, "You boys think keeping your identity secret's going to make any difference?'

Mack sneered at Pete. 'I just told you; go ahead an' get out your ropes.'

Jason reached over and tapped Mack on the chest. 'No one's going to lynch you, but if you're smart you'll answer questions when they're asked.'

Mack sneered again. 'Or?' he said.

Jason's big fist balled up several inches below Mack's nose. 'Or,' old Jason said mildly, 'I'll show you how the Injuns half

171

kill a man with their hands, and never leave
a mark on the outside o' his hide.'

Mack considered that formidable fist a
moment then looked at his companion.
The other man looked straight back, saying
nothing. Mack then said, 'Where's the other
feller who was with us? His horse fell back up
in those lousy rocks. You fellers nail him?'

Doc nodded. 'We nailed him. Now I think
you'd better answer the question: Who are
you men; what're you doing in the McAllister
country?'

Mack looked at Jason again. Every man
around him was waiting. He had no recourse
anyway; he was disarmed, defeated, and on
foot. If anything ever spelt demoralization for
a nightrider, it was the combination of those
particular factors.

'McAuliffe,' he said sulkily. 'I'm Mack
McAuliffe. That feller over there's Carl
Seaver.' He raised his bitter eyes. 'The feller
you nailed back in those lousy hills was Slim
Sutliff. Them names mean anything to you?'

Doc nodded. None of the others so much
as batted an eyelid. 'We get the newspapers
in McAllister,' said Doc dryly. 'You men
killed three people in a bank robbery down
in Oregon City a month or so back.'

Mack's lip curled disdainfully. 'You don't
get very many newspapers,' he said, 'if that's
all you've read about us.'

Frank Hall spat aside and raised bleak eyes.

'Start walkin',' he said. 'It's a long way back to town.' He looked over at Palmer. 'Jess; you still got a horse. Ride on back and fetch us out some more animals. We'll walk along until you get back out here.'

McAuliffe swore. 'I ain't walkin,' he snapped. 'If you fellers figure to take me back to . . .'

'A couple of hours ago,' interrupted Doc Heatly calmly, 'you ran onto a couple of rangeriders. Did you shoot at them?'

McAuliffe blinked at this abrupt change in the conversation. 'Shoot at them?' he repeated. 'Hell no we didn't shoot at them. What d'you think we are, idiots? If we'd shot at them you'd have known which way we were going. We saw them and made a run on them. We wanted their horses, but we didn't fire off a shot. You'd have heard it if we had.'

Doc turned as Jessica walked up. She didn't say anything although her expression was questioning. It was Jason who spoke next, saying to Doc and the others, 'I was mistaken about Connery and that other feller back there. I'm glad to admit it, for their sake.'

Jess walked away lugging his carbine, which he'd retrieved from a bush where he'd evidently left it prior to stalking in close to the outlaws with Frank. The others stood around eyeing their prisoners. Frank said, 'McAuliffe; what exactly were you men

173

trying to do, back there in that blind canyon?'

'Trying to get back to Montana,' said Mack. 'That feller you killed up in the pass came from there. He said he knew all the country between Oregon City and the Montana highlands, too, the louse; then he let us get bottled up in a damned dead-end canyon. I figure, if you fellers hadn't killed Slim, Carl and I would've, eventually.'

'Did Sutliff leave a bedroll blanket behind, when you fellers left the canyon and ran for it?' asked Doc.

McAuliffe grinned. 'Sure; we figured you fellers'd find it, too. But that simple-minded Sutliff forgot about the stencil on the blanket until we were ten miles off. That was another reason for shootin' him; only neither I nor Carl knew these Idaho hills at all, so we kept still an' let him lead us on through. Only it didn't work out that way, did it?'

Doc didn't answer. He turned when Jessica plucked his sleeve, and started walking back to the buggy with her. Seaver, who'd been silent most of the time up to now, said, gazing at Frank Hall. 'Do you Idaho fellers always put your posses in buggies?'

Frank didn't answer. He jerked his head and reached over to give McAuliffe a rough shove. Jess was gone. Only Jason still had a horse to ride. Pierson looked out over the steely dawn and muttered an oath under his breath. It was a long, long way back to town;

174

he didn't like to walk; never had liked to walk, and for that matter never walked at all if he could avoid it. But this time he couldn't very well get out of it, so he fell in beside Frank and started trudging along.

Over at their buggy Jessica and Doc climbed up and eased back for just a moment, saying nothing, letting the built-up tensions slowly atrophy. Finally, as Doc leaned, and pushed his carbine down into the boot which was strapped to the dashboard, Jessica also leaned and unwound the lines, evened them in her hands and gave them a light flick. The harness-horse leaned into his breast-collar, started the rig moving, pointed his nose in the general direction of town and went thoughtlessly pacing along.

Doc said, 'Jess; no one asked McAuliffe what became of that Oregon City bank money.'

'There'll be time,' she murmured. 'How do you feel?'

'Well; about like a fat man who's just been yanked through a knothole, I guess.'

'You were lucky, George. We were all lucky. I can think of several others who weren't so lucky.'

Doc nodded, thinking of Fred Coffey and Randy Collins, that unknown rangeman McAuliffe and Seaver had wantonly shot down up near the pass for no reason at all except that in their flight they'd stumbled

175

upon him. And finally, he thought of the dead outlaw up there in the rocks where the pass led downward from that high-country big meadow.

Jessica said, 'I told you; it's a nightrider's moon. Look over there where it's paling out.'

Doc didn't look. Reaction was setting in for him; he was having to fight to keep his eyes open at all, and that gun round his middle not only gouged him, but its solid weight dragged at him too. He unbuckled the shell-belt and dropped the thing on the floorboards.

'Jessica; I'm bushed. But before I drop off I'd like to ask you to marry me. It's good to get things caught up and set in orderly sequence before a man goes to sleep.'

She smiled. 'You go ahead and sleep,' she murmured. 'I'll drive through the dawn and think about marrying you.'

That wasn't the correct answer; it certainly wasn't the answer he'd anticipated, so he sat straight up and blinked several times to bring himself back to full wakefulness, then he turned, winced, and studied her profile for a moment. In the brightening glow of a new day her flesh was golden, her hair wonderfully heavy and long, the rise and fall of her breasts tantalising, and the proud set of her rounded chin and jaw something for a man to think back on in other years, remembering their strength and beauty.

'You kissed me last night,' he said.

She still had a little hint of a smile down around her heavy mouth. 'Did I, George? Does that mean I'll marry you?'

'Well confound it,' he retorted, sitting up even straighter. 'It means *something*. Beautiful women don't go around kissing men unless . . .'

'Unless they feel sorry for them, or sad for them, or grateful to them, or warm towards them, or . . .'

'All right, all right,' he exclaimed, breaking in. 'But we talked of marriage. You remember that, surely.'

She nodded. 'I remember.' She turned, her green eyes misty. 'I was teasing you. A woman only gets asked to marry a man once in her lifetime. At least that's how I've been raised to believe. You can't blame me for wanting to prolong the moment, can you, George?'

He eased back again and closed his eyes. 'No. Anyway, I wouldn't blame you. But is it settled?'

'It's settled. I'll marry you whenever you wish.'

He started to say: 'When we get back to . . .' and fell asleep before he finished it.

She put both the lines in one hand, raised a sturdy arm and drew him over to her. She brushed his whiskery lips with her mouth then settled him comfortably against her shoulder and settled back to drive like that without seeing her father approaching from the off side

177

until he reined in close and his big shadow fell across one side of the rig.

She looked up and smiled. Old Jason didn't smile back but he studied them both for a while then said, 'Jess; I've seen how you looked at that one. You pity him because he's hurt.'

'He wasn't hurt yesterday, Paw, when they rode into the yard, and I knew when I saw him, even then.'

Jason looked at the steel sky, at the onward plain, at the sleeping medical man beside his lovely daughter again. 'It's been a bad night, Jess,' he murmured. 'What we all need is a lot of rest. Then we can think straighter.'

'I'm not tired, Paw, Not now. I was while we were going back and forth looking for those nightriders. Tired and sad and discouraged. But right now . . . I feel good all over.'

'Jess; you don't know this man. Besides; he's not a very good rider and he's certainly no stockman.'

'He's a doctor, Paw. He heals folks. He believes like you believe; that a man should try living good if his enemies'll let him. But if they won't . . .' she shrugged and traded a long, sober look with old Jason. 'He killed one of them up at the pass, didn't he? And he never quit even after he'd been hurt so badly he could hardly walk.'

Jason still stubbornly rode along, his black gaze unrelenting, his massive jaw locked down

178

in powerful resistance.

Jessica said: 'Paw . . . ?'

'Yes, girl.'

'I told him I'd marry him.'

Jason looked shocked. 'Before he even asked you, girl?'

'No. He asked me.'

Jason's expression altered but unless one watched his eyes it was difficult to tell in that weak, bluish light, with his full beard splayed out concealing most of his face. He rode along for nearly a quarter of a mile, then all he said was, 'I'd best drift on back and see how Frank and that saloonman are making out.'

Jessica watched him drop back, then turn. She was still looking after him when she murmured, 'You can open your eyes now, he's gone.'

George sat up. 'How did you know I was awake?'

She smiled into his eyes. 'If I'm going to be your wife I should know things like when you're asleep and when you're awake, shouldn't I?'

George yawned, rubbed the back of his neck and said, 'Someday you and I are going to have a little talk.'

She nodded agreeably. 'All right. Is tomorrow too soon?'

'Next year may be too soon,' he muttered, and dropped over against her shoulder again. 'I'm going to sleep for a year.'

She reached up, brushed aside his hair and kissed him. Then she said, 'Care to bet on that, George?'

CHAPTER EIGHTEEN

Jess Palmer met them two miles closer to town, but he didn't just bring back horses, he also brought back Dave Miller in a surrey and four armed townsmen to help old Jess lead the spare horses. Pete Pierson put a jaundiced gaze upon Jess and wanted to know what had taken him so long. Otherwise, though, everyone was pleased to affect this meeting, except Seaver and McAuliffe, who were unceremoniously pushed into Miller's surrey with their wrists lashed behind their backs. Mack complained once, on the drive back, that Miller was deliberately going out of his way to hit the bumps and wallows. Up front, riding sideways so that he could see the prisoners at all times, Pete Pierson said he thought Dave was doing that, too, and he blandly smiled at the murderers of Sheriff Fred Coffey.

When they reached town Frank, Jason, Pete, Jess Palmer and Doc got a bad jolt. There was a large, silent torchlight reception committee. It consisted exclusively of men with rifles and shotguns and carbines, as well as beltguns. No one said a word as the riders came wearily up through town. Jessica drove the buggy she and Doc had used, behind the surrey and team Dave Miller was tooling. She and Doc looked along both sides of the roadway where that silent, still and motionless mob of armed men stood, watching grimly as Miller's surrey went past, their faces hard and coppery under their up-held torches.

Lynch mob!

Frank Hall, Jess and Jason were on horseback. Doc twisted on the seat to look around for them. They were back there with the four riders who'd come out with Jess, and in that reddish light Doc could see how their expressions were changing as they too saw the kind of a reception that was awaiting them—and the prisoners.

Doc straightened up and gazed ahead where Dave Miller was driving his team. Miller knew about all this! He wasn't going to stop at the jailhouse at all; he was going to drive right past it. Doc made a fast decision. He knew that if this determined mob ever got their hands on McAuliffe and Seaver no amount of remonstrating was going to get them away from those lynchers alive.

He looked ahead. They were coming close to Fred Coffey's dark and empty jailhouse. He wondered if the front door was unlocked and hoped mightily that it would be, then he leaned over and told Jessica to break out and around the surrey so that she could force it over to the tie-rack in front of the jailhouse.

She looked at him from a pale face, and wordlessly nodded. She understood. Doc craned backwards once more. Jason and Frank were urging their mounts on up towards the surrey, evidently with some notion of their own in mind. Doc waited, letting them come alongside on the right and left of his buggy, then leaned out and beckoned Frank down from his saddle. As Hall leaned Doc told him swiftly what he was going to try. He didn't have to elaborate because Jessica suddenly flicked her lines and swung the buggy outwards and forwards. Frank nodded at Doc and grimly straightened back upright in his saddle. Doc watched Frank's face until he could no longer do that without twisting completely around, trying to gauge Hall's reaction. He was recalling Frank's remarks to old Jason which had favoured, or at least had *seemed* to favour, lynching Fred Coffey's killers. Now; he hoped Frank wouldn't go over to the side of the mob. If that happened, knowing what Doc intended to try, Frank could circumvent Doc's scheme. And yet Doc needed Frank exactly as he needed Pete and Jess Palmer and old Jason. That was a large, ugly mob lining the roadway, and very clearly Dave Miller was sympathetic towards its intentions, which probably meant that those men farther back who'd come out with Jess and Dave to where Doc and his companions had the captives, were probably also part of the mob.

Jessica drove up beside the surrey. Dave Miller turned to gaze over at her. So did Pete Pierson and the prisoners. She flicked the lines and urged her buggy animal on ahead. Miller evidently thought only that she meant to get ahead of him; to lead the cavalcade. It didn't dawn on him until she was forcing his team of handsome sorrel horses over towards the plank kerbing that she had something altogether different in mind. Then he called to her irritably to give way. She didn't give an inch and Miller, in order to avoid a tangle, drew hard on his left line swinging his team in towards the jailhouse tie-rack.

Doc got down and skip-hopped swiftly over to the surrey. 'Get 'em inside, quick,' he told Pierson. 'Move, dammit, Pete!'

Pierson was staring at Doc. Dave Miller suddenly understood. He leaned down. 'Doc; Coffey's dead. We're the law in McAllister now. Don't make folks change their opinion of you. Right now they figure you're a hero. Let it go like that.'

Frank Hall rode up on Miller's side of the surrey, leaned from the saddle and pushed a sixgun into Dave's neck. 'Get down,' he growled. 'Miller; get out of there and shut up. Not another word out of you.'

Doc jerked his head at the prisoners. 'Get out on the far side,' he snapped, 'and get inside that jailhouse. This is a lynch mob out here. Move fast; they're starting to come over here. *Move!*'

Pierson was still stunned, but neither Seaver nor McAuliffe needed a second command to alight and run for the jailhouse. But the second they hit the ground, moving awkwardly because of their bound arms, the crowd began to make a low growl and come towards them, torches held high, guns bristling, faces fierce and adamant in the flickering, red glare.

Jason sprang down from his saddle and moved swiftly to get between the nightriders and the nearest lynchers. He was a head taller and an axe-handle thicker than the nearest men; when they rushed forward he settled himself squarely in their path, legs wide, huge fists balled and ready, black eyes and streaked beard grimly turned upon them. The foremost lynchers faltered. That was all the time Pete and Frank needed to push the prisoners into the jailhouse. Old Jess was trying to shoulder through the crowd to assist his friends, but he didn't make it; at least he didn't get up there in front of the jailhouse until the oaken door was slammed from within, and barred.

Jason relaxed and stepped back with Doc, putting his mighty shoulders to the rough front wall of the jailhouse. He looked broodingly hard and unrelenting as the first wave of those growling, armed men came up and halted, glaring at both Jason and Doc.

184

Dave Miller was standing out there beside his surrey. He said, 'Doc; don't try stoppin' things. We planned this right after you fellers left town tonight. We're the law now. Fred's dead and the Town Council hasn't appointed anyone to take his place. Listen Doc; tomorrow we'll have another sheriff. From tomorrow on everything'll be handled legal-like. But tonight—what's left of tonight anyway—we got our duty to do. Don't spoil things, Doc.'

The crowd muttered approval of Miller's words. Then old Jason rumbled out at them, shaking a mighty fist in their faces. 'You'll be no better than McAuliffe and Seaver. You know very well Fred Coffey'd turn over in his grave if he could see you now—his friends and neighbours. Fred Coffey wouldn't have allowed this. You're no lawmen, you're a pack of yellow wolves, trying to tear down what other men have done, which was right and just.' Jason lowered his fist. 'All right; prove that you're as lawless as McAuliffe and Seaver. Prove it; I dare you! Shoot me where I stand in front of this door, because that's the only way you're going to get past me to take those men out and lynch them.' He rolled his big head from side to side, glaring black defiance. 'Shoot, damn you,' he bellowed. '*Shoot!*'

The crowd fell silent. Torches burned and men held their guns pointing forward. No one moved nor spoke a word. Out by his surrey

185

Dave Miller said in a soft tone of voice, 'Doc; we got the right to hang them. They'll hang anyway. You know that.' But Miller's voice lacked conviction.

Doc answered in the same quiet manner. He said, 'They'll hang, Dave, sure. But that's for the law to do, not you fellers. If you're so dead set on watching them hang, just be patient for a week or two, until the circuit judge gets down here and tries them. Sure they'll hang, but legally, and it won't be on your conscience or mine, or anyone else's, that we leaned on the rope.'

The crowd shifted a little; here and there an armed man grounded his rifle or carbine or shotgun to lean upon it and gaze around. The fire was dying out of the thing; the ferocity and willingness to do murder was cooling out. Behind Doc and old Jason the jailhouse door swung back and Frank Hall appeared in the opening, tall, lean, bronzed and hard-eyed.

'Doc's right, boys,' he said. 'You're not coming in here unless you kill the men who hunted down Fred Coffey's killers and brought them back here.' Frank pointed out where Jessica sat unnaturally erect in the buggy. 'You'll have to kill her too, boys. She did as much as any man to get these killers back here. 'You got any stomach for shootin' down a girl?'

The crowd made a low murmur, almost like a low wail in which no particular words were distinguishable. Some of the angry men began to turn away. Near the rear of the crowd a man dropped his firebrand and stamped on it, then set his back to the others and walked away. One or two other armed men also left the crowd; they weren't many at first, but their departure completed the demoralization. Eventually all of them shuffled their feet, looked at one another, then also turned their backs on the jailhouse.

Agnes Carlisle walked over to the buggy and said something up to Jessica. Jason's daughter nodded, looped the lines and stiffly alighted. Aggie put an arm around her waist. Doc and Jason and Frank watched those two slow-pacing their way over towards Aggie's building across the roadway.

Doc let his breath out slowly and turned. Frank said, 'Come on inside; Fred's old coffee pot's still on the stove.'

McAuliffe and Seaver were over against the far wall pale and haunted looking. Mack said, as the men stepped inside and closed the door. 'That was damned close.' He sounded badly shaken and enormously relieved. No one answered him. No one even looked over at him.

Frank and Jess Palmer got the stove going and filled Sheriff Coffey's graniteware pot with water from the pail nearby. Pete Pierson leaned aside his carbine, barred the roadway door and sank down upon a bench.

187

Jason stepped to a small, grilled front window and gazed out into the dark roadway. Across from the jailhouse there was a yellow glow over at Aggie's place. He said, 'Who was that woman?'

Doc, easing gingerly down in front of the dead sheriff's desk, told him who Agnes Carlisle was. He also said Jessica couldn't be in better hands, so old Jason turned away from the window, sought a chair, and sank down upon it. He gazed around the room, his thoughts fairly obvious. This was a motley crew he was with tonight, and yet, despite all their wide differences, in the things that counted they had proven themselves worthwhile men in every way.

Frank Hall found a pony of rye whiskey in a drawer and measured out a little into each tin cup, but before he filled the last one he held the bottle a moment and looked inquiringly over at Jason.

'It's a tonic,' he said. 'Not many things in this world are bad until men start making them bad. How about it, Jason; a little tonic in your cup?'

Jason nodded gravely. 'I'd like that, Frank, an' what you just said is the gospel truth. Nothing much in this world is really bad until men make it so.'

There was a copper key-ring on Coffey's desk which Doc picked up and tossed over at Jess Palmer. 'Lock those two in the cells,'

188

he said. 'It'll sour my coffee having to sit here looking at them.'

Jess moved at once to obey. As McAuliffe and Seaver were herded through the rear-wall doorway into the cell-block, all the men sitting and standing in the outer office turned to watch them pass from sight. No one said anything but all of them had their private thoughts.

Frank didn't wait for the coffee to get hot. He began pouring it into the tin cups when it was only luke-warm, but to men who'd been as long without anything to eat or drink as those men had been, it tasted good; especially since it was liberally laced.

Doc raised his cup in a little salute. 'To Collins and Coffey, and that dead one out there at the foot of the pass,' he said. They all lifted their cups, then drank. For a moment afterwards old Jason gazed into his cup, deep in thought. It was very quiet now; outside, McAllister slumbered; inside, the quiet was thick and deep.

Old Jason raised his cup. 'To Doctor Heatly,' he said, 'and Jessica. A man always knows that someday, when he raises a daughter, she'll pick her mate and leave home. I reckon most fathers don't get the chance to see how their prospective sons-in-law'll act under stress and peril, so they just sort of have to accept them on blind faith. Well; I'm luckier'n that. We sure may have our differences—me'n Doctor Heatly—but he's a man clear through. A father can't ask more'n that, can he?'

They raised their cups in Doc's direction, then drained off their laced coffee. It made them feel better almost at once. Frank drew forth his watch, opened the case and said, 'Two o'clock in the morning, boys. I reckon we might as well head for home and get what sleep we can for the balance o' this night.'

Doc got up, crossed to the door, opened it and gazed up and down the dark, empty roadway. He said, 'Come along, Jason. You'll stay up at my place. I've got an extra bedroom.' Then he limped outside and paused to lift his head and gaze up where that lowering moon hung softly in its purple setting. The Nightrider's Moon, Jessica had called it.

Jason came out to him. They wordlessly turned and started walking northward.